The Unwilling Executive (Captured by Love Book 1)

Miranda P. Charles

Published by: MPC Romance Publishing

ISBN-13: 978-1508684664
ISBN-10: 1508684669

http://www.mirandapcharles.com

The Unwilling Executive (Captured by Love Book 1)

CHAPTER ONE

Jade Tully exhaled her frustration as she checked her watch for the umpteenth time. It was thirty-five minutes past the scheduled start of her meeting with a guy called Lucas Renner, and he still hadn't turned up.

She drummed her fingers on the wooden table of the busy café in the middle of Sydney's bustling business district while surveying the patrons. Perhaps Lucas was already here, waiting?

No. She was the only one sitting by herself.

Unfortunately, she didn't even know what Lucas looked like. She was relying on her new boss's assurance that Lucas would get the message of where she was sitting and the colour of the top she was wearing.

"Can I take this for you?" a wait staff asked, indicating her empty mug.

"Yes, thank you," she answered. "And I'll have another latté, please. Decaf, this time."

"Sure."

Jade didn't want another drink, but the establishment was full and she felt guilty hogging a table when there were people waiting for a seat. She grabbed her phone and dialled the direct line for Thomas Bilton.

"Jade," her employer answered.

"Hello, Mr. Bilton. I just want you to know I'm still waiting for Mr. Renner. He hasn't turned up yet."

"Hang on a minute. Let me check if he's left a message."

A few seconds later, Thomas was back on the line.

"There are no messages, Jade. Please keep waiting. He must be held up somewhere."

"Okay, sir."

"Jade, remember it's of utmost importance that you get him to read the letter and get his answer. And as I've said before, don't worry if he gets annoyed. He'll be reacting to the message, not to you. Okay?"

"Yes, sir," she answered, her curiosity spiking once again.

Thomas hadn't told her anything about this errand, except to say that it was a private but extremely important matter. So she didn't press for more information. Anyway, how hard could it be to get someone to read a letter and get an answer?

She took out a sealed envelope from her handbag and inspected it again. Not even the recipient's name was on it.

It was all very strange, and she couldn't help but think that this extraordinary task demonstrated Thomas Bilton's eccentric tendencies that Lexie Mead, one of her best friends, had told her about.

Lexie worked in the marketing department at Bilton Machineries and had witnessed some of the odd demands Thomas had made to their team. Evidently though, Thomas had always known what he was doing. After all, the man had single-handedly built a construction machinery company in Australia that now had branches in several countries.

Who knew, maybe Thomas and Lucas Renner were partners in a top-secret project, and they didn't trust email technology for delivering important documents.

Jade rolled her eyes at herself. Gosh, she was so bored with waiting that she was coming up with ridiculous ideas. In all probability, this assignment might be her boss's way of testing to see if she was indeed the best person to be his new PA.

Lexie had nominated her for the position when Thomas' long-serving employee had retired last week. Aided by a glowing reference from her old boss, Jade was the last person standing after a gruelling selection process.

The job offer came at the right time. Jade was still in shock from her previous employer selling the company to an overseas buyer, who'd subsequently closed the Australian branch. Heaven knew she needed a good salary to help her older brother Jerry and his wife with their financial needs. Their baby boy had just had open-heart surgery to fix a congenital birth defect and was in for years of medical care. Even though Jerry didn't like taking money from Jade, it wasn't a matter of choice.

But Jade wasn't guaranteed to keep this new job. She was on the usual three-month probationary period, and Thomas had made it clear that if she didn't perform to expectations, she'd be replaced immediately.

So it bothered her that Lucas Renner still hadn't turned up. Damn it. Another important task waited for her in the office—one she was supposed to finish before she went home for the day. It was taking her longer than expected to complete because she was still learning the system.

A commotion outside drew her attention. Someone must have knocked down a lady, who was now gathering what looked like pamphlets from the ground—chasing after some that were being blown by the breeze. Passers-by helped, and a tall, dark-haired man caught Jade's eye.

He was good-looking. Extremely.

The guy turned his back to her as he stooped down to pick up a loose sheet. While he was wearing a business shirt, she could already picture a hard and muscular body underneath his clothes. He was pure male from the way he moved.

Jade rested her chin on her hands and continued to watch, enjoying her unexpected reaction to the stranger. It had been such a long time since someone attracted her enough to make her want to gape.

A gust of wind blew the paper he was trying to retrieve, causing Mr. Hot to face her way again.

Suddenly, he glanced up and caught her staring at him through the window.

Jade's eyes widened before she found herself hastily averting her gaze up towards the ceiling, as if something there had captured her attention.

She almost laughed out loud when she realised what she'd done. Wow, she couldn't remember the last time she'd behaved like that from being caught ogling.

A wait staff delivered her second latté. She smiled her thanks before looking out the window again. But Mr. Hot was nowhere to be seen.

Ah, damn. Why couldn't she have smiled at him? She wasn't shy around men.

She smirked. No she wasn't usually shy unless the guy was really attractive—as in *incredibly*. Then she got flustered—an irritating reaction she'd been trying to change. But it hadn't been easy making improvements in that area when she hardly stumbled across such men. She guessed she had 'high standards' when it came to who could make her blush.

Well, considering her luck with men, Mr. Hot was probably already taken anyway.

"Hi."

Jade's heart fluttered as she glanced up. Mr. Hot wasn't outside because he was inside.

"Hi," she responded.

"Jade Tully?"

Her jaw dropped. "Yes."

"I apologise for being so late. I'm Lucas Renner."

What? She'd expected to meet with a man close to her boss's age of sixty-four. But the hunk in front of her seemed no older than thirty—about five years older than her, if she wasn't mistaken.

"Seeing how tardy I've been, I can understand why you're reluctant to shake my hand," Mr. Hot said, his tone apologetic and teasing at the same time. It was kind of cute.

"Hi, Mr. Renner," she said, rousing her addled brain and going for the handshake while her face burned. Ugh. Did she have to blush?

"Please call me Lucas," he said as he sat on the chair opposite her. "I'm really sorry for making you wait. I was at another meeting that took much longer than expected. I didn't have your contact details so I couldn't update you. But thanks so much for waiting."

"No problem," she responded, her earlier annoyance dissipating. His excuse was understandable, she guessed.

A wait staff approached and offered Lucas a menu.

"What else would you like, Jade?" he asked.

"Oh, I'm fine, thanks."

"Are you sure? I made you wait for so long that I owe you at least a cake or coffee. Please have another one with me," Lucas said, smiling.

Her lips curved up in response. "Maybe I'll have sparkling mineral water then."

"Just that?"

"Yes, thanks."

"Don't you want something sweet to go with it?" Lucas asked, cocking his head to the side.

Was it her imagination or did Lucas' tone drop a tad? And was that a flirtatious look he was giving her?

"Just that," she said, taking a deep breath.

Lucas gave his order to the waitress, then leaned on the table, a charming smile still on his face.

"So, Jade, you're here to interview me about my work?" Lucas said.

Jade's eyebrows shot up in surprise. "Uh, no. I'm here to hand you this letter."

Lucas frowned as he took the envelope from her. "Are these the interview questions?"

"I don't know, actually. I was just told to give it to you and ask you to read it." She fidgeted in her seat, getting uncomfortable. What the hell was this about?

Lucas tore the envelope open and pulled out a sheet of paper.

In a second, his friendly countenance disappeared, replaced by a glare of displeasure.

Eek.

*****

Lucas stared at the signature line of the printed letter. Scrawled in black ink were three unmistakable words: *Your father, Thomas.*

Heat rose to his face and he didn't bother hiding his scowl.

"This is from Thomas Bilton," he said accusingly to the brunette in front of him.

"Yes," Jade said with a hint of apprehension. "I'm his new PA."

"I don't appreciate being conned like this," he rasped, slitting his eyes.

"Conned? I don't understand," she said, her eyes rounding.

He crumpled the sheet and put it in his pocket. "Did you type the letter?" he grunted as he took a couple of bills from his wallet and dropped them on the table.

"No. Mr. Bilton must have typed it himself," Jade answered, sounding nervous. "I don't know anything about it. He just told me to come here and hand it to you."

He inhaled deeply, scrutinising Jade. She held his gaze, looking bewildered… and damned attractive. It was a pity she worked for Thomas Bilton.

"I wouldn't have turned up if I knew this was Bilton's doing," he said, standing up. "I don't mean to be rude, but I'm leaving now."

"Wait, Lucas, please," Jade said, rising to her feet. "Could you please just read it? I'm supposed to relay your answer back to Mr. Bilton."

He snorted.

"Please, Lucas," she said quietly. "He told me it's imperative that you read it."

Something in Jade's tone made Lucas pause, and he found himself pulling the letter out and smoothing it. Admittedly, this whole business of a beautiful woman hand-delivering him a letter made him curious as to its contents.

He read it and his lips twisted. The old man was good. He penned quite a moving piece—if Lucas didn't know any better. But he did. Thomas Bilton was simply trying to manipulate him to protect his reputation.

He shoved the paper back in his pocket. "You said you don't know what this is all about?"

Jade shook her head.

"So if your boss tells you to jump off a cliff, you'd do it without any question?"

Jade's face reddened. "Of course not. I didn't ask questions because he said it was a private matter."

"So you're the kind of person who doesn't care if your job requires you to lie, as long as you get paid good money for it." Why he felt the need to goad the truth out of her, he didn't know.

Jade lifted her chin up in defiance. "I'm sorry, but I never lied to you. I was simply following instructions to meet you."

They glared at each other, and Lucas felt his anger start to evaporate. Jade's expression seemed honest enough. And hell, her captivating face was distracting him.

Those long lashes that framed her beautiful hazel eyes didn't seem embellished by mascara. And her lips—full and sexy, and—

"I need your answer, Lucas," Jade said.

The bitter taste came rushing back in his mouth. "My answer is no. And if the circumstances were different, I would have said it was a pleasure meeting you, Jade Tully."

Then he walked off.

*

Lucas entered the Bondi car service centre owned by his close friend, Connor Reid. He walked to the state-of-the-art service area at the back and found Connor there, checking a computer monitor that gave the condition of one of his client's vehicles.

"Hey, bro," Connor said. "How was your meeting with Jade what's-her-name?"

"She was a fake," he said flatly.

"What do you mean?"

"She wasn't there to interview me for an article. She's Thomas Bilton's PA."

Connor stared at him before pressing a button on the screen. Then Connor led him to his office.

Lucas started for the sofa in Connor's big room, but changed his mind and sat on a chair by the desk.

"What's wrong with the couch?" Connor asked.

"Please," he said with snicker. "I'm not going to sit where you and your wife have sex when no one's around."

"Hey, it's been treated with a stain-resistant thing. And Amanda changes the blanket all the time."

"Amanda was here last night while you worked overtime, wasn't she?"

Connor just grinned at him and sat on his chair behind the desk.

Lucas shook his head good-naturedly. There had been a time, when he and Connor had worked for the same Formula One team as mechanics, that the two of them had competed for the title Mr. Fuck King—a label jokingly given to Connor by their workmates because of Connor's popularity with women from different parts of the globe. Now the title was all Lucas', but it had lost its lustre. He'd only wanted it for the fun of stripping it away from Connor, anyway.

A picture of Jade Tully popped into his head. Unfortunately, it came with the remembrance of whom she worked for.

"So this Jade woman was sent by Thomas to talk to you?" Connor asked.

"Yup. She made me read this letter where Thomas pleaded for me to talk about the possibility of being part of Bilton Machineries. He said he's getting old and wants to make sure that the company continues to be owned and operated by his own flesh and blood. And since I'm his sole *heir*..." He couldn't help but say the last word with a good dose of sarcasm.

"And you still don't want to have anything to do with the company? Or him?" Connor asked gently.

"Come on, bro. You know the whole story. Why would he want me to run his company?"

"Hey, you're the one responsible for making your mother's flower shop a success because you made sure she has efficient systems for online ordering and fast delivery. Sure, there's a difference between a flower shop and a billion-dollar company, but—"

"That's not what I mean, Connor," he interrupted. "This is all a joke. Thomas never acknowledged me as his son, much less his heir, until recently. He's up to something."

"Okay, fine," Connor said, raising his arms in surrender. "So did you tell off that Jade woman for lying?"

Lucas sighed, Jade Tully's apprehensive but beautiful face appearing in his mind. "I don't blame her. I'm sure she was just following Thomas' orders. She's new, so she must be desperate to keep her job."

"You have to admit she was effective," Connor commented. "How many times did the other PA try to get you to talk to Thomas, or read the emails and letters she sent for him?"

"Yeah," Lucas said, wondering if he'd ever cross paths with Jade Tully again.

CHAPTER TWO

Jade stood by the threshold of Thomas Bilton's impressive office, her boss so focused on his computer that he hadn't noticed her standing there. For a man who was almost sixty-five and could retire with more money than Jade would know what to do with, Thomas still worked at least fifty hours a week.

Jade had already experienced how exacting Thomas was as a boss. She didn't mind it. It was actually quite inspiring. In the handful of days that she'd worked for him, she could see why he'd become very successful.

Besides, she'd heard from Lexie how generous Thomas was to his dedicated employees. Jade hoped to be on the receiving end of some eye-popping bonuses, too.

But right now, she wasn't looking forward to the conversation she was about to have with her boss. Contrary to what Lucas had accused, she wasn't someone who did things without question. So even though she'd be risking her boss's ire, she had to say something about the way she'd been kept in the dark about what Lucas had been told. She didn't want to establish a precedent she wasn't comfortable with.

She rapped on the door, making Thomas look up.

"Jade!" Thomas rose from his chair and gazed at her with hopeful anticipation.

Jade hid a sigh as she walked towards her boss's desk.

"Lucas turned up?" Thomas asked, gesturing for her to take a seat.

"Yes, sir," she said, sitting down. "His answer was no. He also said he didn't appreciate being conned—"

Thomas gasped. "He read the letter?"

"Yes. But—"

"He read it?" Thomas asked again in delighted disbelief.

"Yes, and he said no to whatever's in it, sir," she repeated, wondering if her boss hadn't heard her earlier. "But, Mr. Bilton—"

"Oh, Jade. Thank you!"

Jade frowned in confusion.

"This is progress," Thomas said, still looking thrilled. "Do you know how many times I've tried to get him to listen to what I have to say? I sent him emails and tried to call him. But he didn't want to listen to a single word. Then I got other people to intervene on my behalf. Still no success—until now. I don't expect him to have a change of heart from the one letter you handed him, but I'm encouraged that he read it."

Jade took a deep breath. Well, that was an unexpected reaction.

"What did you say to him?" Thomas asked eagerly. "How did you get him to read the whole letter?"

"I pleaded with him, sir," she said with a shrug. "He really wasn't happy, Mr. Bilton. And if you don't mind me saying, I wasn't either. Lucas said he'd been lied to just so he would turn up to our meeting. I would have appreciated if you'd told me that."

"Oh, Jade, I apologise. You see, I needed you to look innocent to boost the chances of his reading the letter. If he got an inkling that it was from me, he wouldn't have opened it. So it worked!"

Jade stared at Thomas. The man was practically glowing, making her ignore her annoyance. Whatever this was about, it was clearly very important to her boss.

Thomas leaned back in his chair. "We must keep on chipping away," he declared.

We?

"I'll need you to get him to talk to you again, Jade. And work on changing his mind."

What?

"I know this is highly unusual," Thomas said. "But I really need your help."

"Sir, after today I doubt he'd want to see or hear from me again."

"Oh, but you must try. You're the first person who's gotten him to pay attention to something from me. And at your first attempt too!"

Jade didn't know what to say.

"You have no idea how important this is to me, Jade," Thomas said quietly. "It's an order."

She sighed. How could she say no when he put it like that? Besides, she'd be lying to herself if she didn't admit that Lucas Renner intrigued her. She wouldn't mind knowing more about him.

"I can only try, Mr. Bilton," she answered. "I can't promise you the results you want."

"And that's all I expect," Thomas replied, beaming at her. "There are things I need to sort out regarding this, and they're taking more time than expected. I'll let you know when I need you to make contact with Lucas again."

"Um, sir, I know you said this is a personal matter. But since I'll be working with you on this, would you mind telling me what this is all about?"

Thomas considered for a moment. "I guess that's a fair request. When I have the information I'm waiting for, we'll talk about it, okay?"

Jade nodded. "Thank you, sir."

"Well, that's it for now. And thank you again, Jade."

"You're welcome, Mr. Bilton."

Jade walked back to her desk, curiosity tickling her hard. Thomas hadn't mentioned a time frame for their conversation, but she'd have to settle for a promise.

*****

Jade entered the apartment she shared with one of her best friends. She lifted her eyebrows when she found Cassie Stephens looking glum as she sat in front of the TV, eating a bar of chocolate.

"Hey, Cassie, what's wrong?" she asked.

"My boss is a prick," Cassie said. "Someone resigned today, and he announced that he won't be looking for a replacement. He expects the rest of us to share the work, but we're already overloaded as it is!"

"I keep telling you to look for another job."

"I'm still waiting for you and Lexie to recommend me for a role at Bilton Machineries," Cassie said with a grin.

Jade chuckled. "Don't worry. We're keeping an eye open for you."

"How was your day?"

"Weird!" Jade sat down to tell her friend about the meeting with Lucas and her conversation with her boss.

"Wow. Sounds very intriguing."

"I know. The best—or worst—part, I'm not sure which yet, was that Lucas Renner is a total hunk."

Cassie lifted an eyebrow. "You met someone today who you think is a total hunk?"

"I looked up at the ceiling as if it were the most interesting thing in the world when he caught me staring at him."

Cassie gasped. "You know what this means. You are *so* interested, Jade Tully."

"Yay. Glad to know my heart hasn't permanently turned to stone after all," she said dryly.

"Yes. Yay," Cassie said, looking pointedly at her. "It's okay to give your heart a rest after it's been hurt. But it's been too long since you've taken a risk in the relationship department, Jade. That's why I think it's exciting that this Lucas guy had a strong effect on you."

"But don't you think it would be totally unprofessional if I flirted with him? Besides, considering his obvious issue with my boss, I doubt he'd even want to be in the same room as me again."

"But didn't Thomas say he wants you to keep *working* on him? Use your charm and see how effective it is," Cassie teased.

"Ha-ha. I don't think my feminine powers would have any effect on him. He's too good-looking," she said with a pout.

"Ah, you are most definitely interested."

"You should have seen him, Cassie. You'd know what I mean. But then again, I think I'll keep him to myself."

"Now you're really making me curious about this guy. Maybe the next time you have to meet with him, I could lurk in the background."

Jade sighed. "Then he'll see you and fall for you. And there goes another guy stolen from me by a so-called friend."

"Excuse me. How dare you think I'm like that woman you used to call friend?" Cassie said, giving her a censuring push. "But... if this Lucas Renner is as hot as you say he is..."

They chortled.

"Glad you're able to laugh at that joke, Jade," Cassie said quietly.

"Yeah. I guess I'm really ready to move on now," she said with a grin, Lucas Renner's handsome face floating in her mind.

*****

"Jade, I know it's late in the day but I need you to do something for me before you leave for home," Thomas said over the phone.

"Sure, Mr. Bilton," Jade answered.

"My wife's niece just had a baby girl. We'll be visiting her in the hospital tonight, and Diana and I want to

21

bring a big bunch of flowers and some gifts for the newborn. Could you get them, please?"

"Of course," she answered. "Do you have a particular gift in mind?"

"Diana's niece had hinted that a bracelet engraved with her child's name would be nice, along with some clothes and toys. You can get the bracelet from our favourite jewellers." Thomas gave her the name of an exclusive store.

"What's the budget, sir?" she asked.

Thomas told her.

Jade gulped. Her most expensive necklace was less than half the price of the bracelet Thomas wanted her to buy.

*

Jade walked towards a flower shop two blocks away, carrying a large shopping bag full of baby stuff. The expensive bracelet she'd just bought was safe in her handbag.

Ruby, the florist, would be surprised to see her back again so soon. She'd been there just last week.

Since her nephew had been diagnosed with a heart condition, Jade had been buying flowers every two weeks for her brother and sister-in-law. At first, Jerry had asked her not to waste money on things that wilted and got thrown away after several days. But the lovely blossoms cheered his wife so much that sometimes Jerry would even remind Jade to pick up a fresh bunch on her way home. Good thing that Ruby had been giving her a good discount for being a frequent customer.

Jade used to buy from a different florist, but when Cassie came home one night with flowers from her workmates for her birthday, Jade had started buying from Ruby. Ruby's arrangements were much more beautiful and the quality of her flowers was superb. She'd been a regular of Ruby's now for over four months and had developed a friendship with the older woman. Ruby had been an additional source of comfort when Jade had been so worried about her nephew's heart surgery.

Jade walked into the inviting flower shop, spotting Ruby with another customer. Her assistant wasn't around, so Jade put the shopping bag down in a corner and browsed the greeting cards section while she waited. Thomas hadn't asked her to buy a card, but she'd get one anyway. There were several cute ones for welcoming a new baby girl into the world.

"What are you doing here?" a low growl came from behind her, making her jump and whirl in surprise.

"Lucas!"

Lucas glared at her, looking more pissed off than he'd been when he'd left her at the café yesterday.

"So?" he whispered harshly, his handsome face marred by a deep scowl.

"Um… I'm here to… buy some flowers." She gave herself a mental shake to get back her composure.

"I don't believe you," Lucas said in a soft but angry tone. "Please leave now."

"What? No! I told you I need to buy some flowers," she whispered heatedly, annoyance replacing her earlier fluster. How dare this guy order her about?

"Come with me," Lucas said, grabbing her arm and steering her to the exit.

23

She resisted, frowning at him. What the hell was wrong with this man?

Cheery goodbyes came from Ruby and her customer, then Ruby appeared from around the corner.

"Jade! Hello. I thought it was you," Ruby greeted, looking at her and Lucas with curiosity.

"Hi, Ruby," Jade said, walking away from Lucas with relief. "I need a big bouquet for someone who's just had a baby girl."

"Sure," Ruby said as she lifted her eyebrows at Lucas. "You two know each other?"

"Yes," Lucas answered, smiling at Ruby. "Jade's a friend of a friend. Anyway, Mum, there's something I need to talk to her about first. Excuse us for a while."

Mum? The revelation disconcerted Jade enough that she let Lucas lead her outside.

Lucas faced her when they were far enough away from the entrance to Ruby's shop. "Thomas sent you here, didn't he?" he asked. "What's your assignment this time? To get my mother to talk to him?"

"No!"

"Don't lie, Jade."

Jade gasped indignantly. "I *am* buying flowers for Mr. Bilton, but he *did not* send me here. For your information, I was Ruby's customer way before I started working at Bilton Machineries. And I had absolutely no idea she's your mother, because in the *four* months that I've been coming here every other week, I've never seen you around. So please don't accuse me of a hidden agenda."

Lucas narrowed his eyes, but she held her head high and glared back at him. She might find him attractive enough to get muddled every once in a while, but she refused to get intimidated by this infuriating male—even though her lashes were batting involuntarily despite her anger.

Argh! Damn him for being so good-looking.

The suspicious look in Lucas' eyes disappeared and his lips curved upwards.

Shit. *Jade Tully, you're so freaking obvious.*

"I'm sorry," Lucas said.

Her brows rose.

"You really didn't come here to talk to my mum about Thomas?" Lucas asked.

"No."

"And you didn't know she's my mother?"

"No. How could I have known that, Lucas?"

"Does she know you work for Bilton Machineries?"

She shook her head. "I only just started, so we haven't had the chance to talk about it yet. I'm sure she'll ask where I work now, though. She knew I was looking for a new job."

"Please don't tell her."

"Why not?"

Lucas rubbed his face. "It's a long story, Jade. And it's private."

"In other words, it's none of my business," she said.

Lucas gave her a tight smile that held sadness she was surprised to see. It pricked her conscience and, unthinking, she squeezed his arm in a gesture of comfort.

Whoa. Muscles.

She pulled away, cursing herself for being too touchy-feely towards a man she hardly knew.

"Lucas, I see your mum every two weeks," she said hurriedly. "Unless there's a long line of customers waiting, we usually have a friendly chat. What should I tell her if she asks me?"

"Anything, as long as you don't say you work for Bilton Machineries. It would upset her if she finds out that Thomas is trying to contact me. Please."

There was no sarcasm on Lucas' tone, only a soft plea. She had lots of questions for him and opened her mouth to ask one. But she shut it and nodded instead. Judging from Lucas' stance, Thomas would be more forthcoming with details. She'd have to wait.

"Thank you, Jade. I appreciate this. Let's go back in." Lucas motioned for her to go first.

She headed back to the flower shop, trying to get a fake story clear in her head. She didn't look forward to dishing out fibs to Ruby, but she couldn't find a good enough reason to argue with Lucas' request. Her gut told her it was the way to go for now.

She only hoped she could be convincing. Her expressions and gestures often gave her away even if her words didn't.

CHAPTER THREE

Lucas ran his gaze on Jade's body as she walked ahead of him. How could he not when she had perfect curves—exactly the kind he got hard for? Couple that with her pretty face, and he wasn't at all surprised at the intense attraction he felt for her.

He shook his head, bemused. He was an unashamed flirt who thoroughly enjoyed the game of seduction. Normally, he would be all over Jade by now, but he had to curb his natural predilection. She was one of Thomas' pawns, albeit an innocent one.

What a shame, since it was obvious that Jade was attracted to him, too. She couldn't have faked the dilation of her pupils when she'd stared at him, breathless.

His mother was alone in the shop when they came back. She was sticking colourful blossoms in a wide square box with a special foam base moistened with cut-flower preservatives.

"There you are," Ruby said. "How big do you want this arrangement to be, Jade?"

"Oh, big, please," Jade answered. "I don't have a limited budget today, so please go all out with it. I'm... uh... sharing the cost for this with other people."

"So it's someone close to you who's had the baby?"

"Yes, a good friend of mine," Jade said, then turned to inspect the displays.

The pinking of Jade's cheeks didn't escape Lucas. He bet she was uneasy lying to his mother.

"So how did you two meet?" Ruby asked, looking at him with a glint in her eye.

Lucas hid a snicker. His mother was very much aware that he enjoyed being with women without the emotional attachments. But his mum still nudged 'nice' girls towards him whenever she could.

"I met Jade through a friend," he answered.

"Oh, right. So who's this mutual friend?" Ruby pressed as she worked on the bouquet.

"Rick."

"Rick Donnelly? The Carmichael brothers' cousin?"

"Yes." Lucas glanced at Jade, who had an almost-panicked look on her face. He suppressed his chuckle. Jade would never win a poker game.

"Right," Ruby said absentmindedly as she stared at her arrangement with a critical eye. Murmuring that she needed more baby's breath, she went to the back room where she kept her flower supplies.

"Who are Rick Donnelly and the Carmichael brothers?" Jade whispered to him urgently when his mother was out of earshot.

"Friends of mine."

Jade rolled her eyes. "Obviously."

He chuckled. "You've heard of the Carmichael Corporation, right? The property development company owned by three brothers?"

"You mean those Carmichaels are friends of yours?" Jade asked, impressed. "Of course I've heard of them. Who hasn't? They're on the papers and magazines constantly."

"Yes. And Rick is their cousin."

Lucas was regretting using Rick's name for this particular lie. Rick, who was introduced to him by Connor, was a successful entrepreneur who owned a chain of luxury car dealerships.

Rick also happened to have Thomas Bilton as one of his most important clients.

Surprisingly, he and Rick had developed a deep friendship despite that one uncomfortable fact. But business was business. It wasn't Rick's fault that Thomas chose to do business with him. And besides, Rick had known Thomas for longer than he'd known Lucas.

"But I don't know anything about Rick," Jade said.

"Don't worry. Mum knows that Rick has plenty of female friends. He throws a lot of parties so it's not surprising that we've 'met' in one of them."

Jade huffed. "I hate making things up on the fly."

"It'll be fine. I think Mum's finished with her questions anyway."

"And if she brings up why we went outside to talk?"

"She won't. But if she did… well, make something up."

Jade frowned and crossed her arms, clearly disapproving of the whole thing.

He smiled. Something about her was simply adorable.

Easy, Lucas. Not this one.

Ruby came out of the back room, her hands full.

"Wow, Ruby, you're adding all that?" Jade said. "It'll be so amazing!"

"You have to tell me when it's enough," Ruby said. "I can get carried away and it might get too big."

"Well, you can make the grandest arrangement you've made in a while. I'm sure my friend would love it."

Ruby grinned. "I will, then. Lucas," she said in a low voice. "Could you attend to that man browsing at the front? Just ask him what he wants, please?"

"Sure," Lucas answered, heading to the middle-aged guy and asking if he could help with anything.

Although he didn't work at the store, Lucas was able to answer the man's questions about prices. Apart from improving the setup and systems of the flower shop, he'd also worked on the budget, including pricing for his mother's products.

The customer left, satisfied and promising to come back in three days to buy a big bunch for his wife for their wedding anniversary.

Lucas walked back towards the counter, grinning. If his colleagues at Formula One learnt that he sometimes helped his mother sell flowers, he'd get the ribbing of his life.

"Oh, Jade, that's great! I'll see you there, then!" he heard Ruby say.

"Really?" Jade asked, her eyes rounding in clear surprise—or horror.

"Yes! I've been invited and I'm also supplying the flowers. It will be my first time going to a Carmichael party," Ruby said.

Lucas inhaled sharply. They were talking about the surprise birthday party for Greg Carmichael that was being organised by Greg's girlfriend, Gemma.

"I didn't know you were going to Greg's party, Jade," he said with a quizzical look. How on earth had Jade managed to get herself in this tangle?

"Oh, I'm still not sure if I'll be going," she answered nonchalantly, although Lucas could see dismay on her face. "Rick did ask me to go with him, but I'm not sure if I could make it."

"Please try, Jade," Ruby said excitedly. "It will be nice to have someone I know there. Unfortunately, Lucas won't be attending because he has to work that weekend."

"You'd know plenty of people at the party, Mum," Lucas interjected. "You've already met all of the Carmichaels. And a few of my other friends will be there, too."

"Sure, but I hardly know them, whereas Jade and I already get along well. We could chat with each other since we both won't know many people there. You know how awkward I tend to feel at parties like that, especially since you won't be there."

Lucas glanced at Jade, who looked guilty and apologetic.

"You can't force Jade to go if she doesn't want to, Mum."

"And yet you force me to go," Ruby said dryly.

He sighed. Ruby was still trying to find an excuse not to attend. Oh, he knew she was excited about the party. She was just plain scared about mingling with the wealthy and influential Carmichaels and their friends.

Life had been tough for his mum, not just financially but also emotionally. Thankfully, she was in a much better place now. But she still had the habit of putting herself down and thinking she was a nobody.

Stuff it, he wasn't letting her get away with that mindset again. "Don't even think of pulling out, Mother," he warned.

"I don't think they'd care if I go or not, Lucas."

"Yes, they will care, Mum. Besides, you've already said yes and it would be rude not to turn up."

"What do you think, Jade?" Ruby asked. "Isn't it intimidating to go to a Carmichael party, especially when they hardly know you?"

"Uh… yeah," Jade answered. "But from what I've heard, they're down-to-earth people so I'm pretty sure they'll make you feel welcome. You should go. You'll have fun."

"It would be nice to go…" Ruby said reluctantly.

"But…?" Lucas asked.

Ruby let out a nervous chuckle. "I don't want to look out of place. I just don't relish the thought of being like a wallflower because I have no one to talk to. And I can't imagine myself chatting easily with the other guests. I wouldn't be surprised if they ignored me, anyway. I'm not rich or famous."

Lucas rolled his eyes.

"I hope you'll decide to attend, Jade," Ruby said almost pleadingly. "That would make two of us who won't know many people there."

"I'll let you know if I can," Jade said with a thin smile.

"Yes, please do. And I think this is done," Ruby said, putting the final touches on her arrangement. "Do you like it?"

"It's wonderful. I love it! Now how much do I owe you?" Jade asked as she pulled some cash from her wallet.

"So this..." Ruby murmured, punching some numbers on the cash register. "Plus the card... less your usual twenty percent discount—"

"Oh, no, Ruby. Full price for this one, please," Jade said.

Ruby shook her head and pointed to the amount showing on the screen.

"I insist, Ruby. There are many of us sharing this. We can afford it. Please."

"I take it you've found a new job?" Ruby asked with a pointed look.

Jade chuckled. "Yes. Why do you think I'm dressed in this corporate attire?"

"That's great! I'm glad for you," Ruby said, adjusting the price accordingly and giving Jade the correct change. "Where are you working now?"

"At a software development company where one of my best friends works."

"Oh, right. When did you start?"

Lucas watched the interaction between Jade and his mother with interest. Obviously, the two shared a rapport that had developed over time.

It was funny how coincidence happened when it was least expected. If his mother found out that Jade was working for the man she'd had a fling with thirty years ago, she'd be incredulous. And upset.

"Thank you so much," Jade said as she prepared to leave, picking up a heavy-looking shopping bag before trying to lift the extra-large arrangement.

"Wow, this is so big I can hardly see where I'm going!" Jade said with a laugh. She struggled to balance the flower box with one arm while carrying her shopping bag with the other.

"Are you going home now?" Ruby asked.

"No. I'm going back to the office first."

"Will you be okay?"

"I'll be fine... I think," Jade said, craning her neck to see where she was going.

Lucas shook his head. There was no way Jade could walk far with her load. "We can get it express delivered for you. Your friend should get it in about two to three hours," he said.

Jade gave him a warning look. "No. We want to take it with us to the hospital tonight. And one of my friends drove today, so I only need to get back to the office."

"Why don't you help her, Lucas?" Ruby said. "Carry it for her to her office."

Lucas gulped. Walk Jade to Bilton Machineries headquarters?

"It's okay, Ruby," Jade said hastily. "I'm sure I can manage. I'll see you next week for my usual fortnightly bunch. Bye, guys!"

Jade made her way to the exit, only to bump against the corner of a low table, almost stumbling.

Lucas exhaled gustily and went to take the flowers from her. "I'll walk with you."

"Thanks," Jade said, looking so relieved that he had to smile.

He waited until they had exited the shop when he asked her the question that was confusing him. "How did you and Mum end up talking about Greg Carmichael's surprise birthday party?"

"Oh. She asked if Rick and I see each other often. Off the cuff, I said mostly at parties. Then she asked if I've heard about the surprise party in two months. Stupid me, I assumed it was one of Rick's because you said he holds them often. So I said yes. She got excited and wanted to know if I was invited. After my previous comments, I felt I didn't have a choice but to say yes to that, too. I had no idea that she was talking about Greg Carmichael's birthday."

"You handled it well," he said with a grin.

"See what happens when you make stuff up without knowing all the facts?" Jade asked wryly.

He laughed out loud, then found himself relaxing and engaging in pleasant conversation as they walked together to Jade's office.

Before he knew it, they were at the Bilton Machineries building.

"Do you think you can manage from here?" he asked as they got to the elevators.

"Yes. Thanks so much, Lucas. You're a lifesaver."
Jade took the box of flowers from him.

"Thomas is bound to see Mum's logo on that
box," he said gravely. "Do you think you can cover it up
before he sees it?"

Jade gave him a startled look. "Is that necessary?"

"It would help," he said quietly.

"What would happen if he does notice it?"

"He might recognise it or he might not. But I think
it's best that he doesn't see it at all."

"May I ask why, Lucas?" Jade asked softly.
"Especially when you're asking me to lie and cover things
up?"

He took a deep, ragged breath. "Maybe later,
okay? But I can assure you that Mum would also prefer
that Thomas doesn't find out where you got those from. In
fact, she probably wouldn't have sold them to you if she
knew who'd ordered them."

Jade stared at him, looking like she wanted to
press further. "Okay," she said with a sigh. "I'll see what I
can do to cover up the logo."

"Thank you," he said sincerely.

"I guess I'll see you around, then."

"Yeah. Maybe," he said. "I don't often visit
Mum's shop. I was only there today because I'm leaving
for Germany tomorrow."

"Germany?"

"Yeah, for the Formula One race there in a couple
of weeks."

"Wow. You're going to Germany to specifically
watch the race?"

"I work for a Formula One team as a mechanic," he said with an amused frown. "Didn't you know that?"

"Oh. No, I didn't."

"Thomas or my mum didn't tell you?"

"I know nothing, Lucas," Jade said with obvious frustration.

"Right. Well, now you know."

"You're away from home a lot then, I take it."

"I used to be. I'll be back in two weeks, have a short break, then go again. I've started to reduce the number of races I work in this year. My friend Connor and I are in discussions about being partners in his car servicing business."

"So do you only work on fast cars? Or do you also work on slow vehicles like, say, tractors or cranes?"

"Full of questions today, Jade Tully," he said, smiling at her pathetic attempt to find a link between him and Bilton Machineries.

Jade blushed. "Sorry. Between you and Mr. Bilton not telling me anything, I'm bursting with curiosity."

He smirked. "Speaking of Thomas, I better go in case I bump into the man."

"Okay. Thanks again for carrying this beautiful box for me."

"My pleasure." It felt natural to kiss her goodbye on the cheek, so he did. Then he pressed the up button for the lifts before strolling to the exit.

Strange how he didn't have the compulsion to leave the Bilton Machineries building as fast as he could. Just the other day, when he had to walk past the premises, his whole body had tensed. He was pleasantly surprised at how relaxed he felt right now.

Involuntarily, he looked back towards the elevators. Jade was still standing there, watching him. He grinned and waved. She waved back, missing the lift that closed its doors and left without her.

CHAPTER FOUR

Lucas strained to hear Jade above the din created by the crowd in the packed food court. He was kicking himself for his stupid decision to take Jade here for lunch—a detour before he walked her back to her office with a big box of flowers for her officemate celebrating a fiftieth birthday. Surely he could have found a quieter place with speedy enough service that would ensure she got back to work on time?

This was the first time they'd had lunch together, although they'd had coffee last week when they'd bumped into each other at his mother's shop after he came back from Germany.

He'd surprised himself by his actions. He certainly didn't expect wanting to have coffee or lunch with Thomas Bilton's PA. But in both cases he'd found himself simply blurting out the invitations.

Jade was saying something about an open-heart surgery and he mentally shook his head to focus on their conversation.

"Did you say your nephew had a heart operation?" he asked, leaning across the table to hear her better.

"Yes. About three months ago. He's doing well at the moment, so we're very relieved. Would you like to see his picture?"

"Sure," he said. "I just realised that you're the customer-friend with a nephew who has congenital heart defect that Mum talks about often. And the flowers you buy regularly are for your brother and sister-in-law, right?"

"Yup," Jade said, smiling as she scrolled through photos on her phone. "I was such a worrywart when my nephew had the operation. Your mum was a big help in calming my fears. Here he is." She handed him her phone. "Isn't he adorable? His name's Michael but we call him Mickey."

"Yeah, he's really cute," he said, smiling at her. "How old is he?"

"Nine months. Would you like to see more? Just scroll to the next pictures. They're all Mickey."

He chuckled. She was clearly besotted with her nephew. He went to the next photo. It was of Jade beaming at the infant she carried in her arms.

His gaze lingered on her image. He'd been trying hard not to gape at her since meeting her at the shop earlier. But now he allowed himself to enjoy focusing on her face in the photo.

What was it about Jade that pulled him so? He knew other women who'd be considered prettier than her in a conventional sense. He'd even had sex with plenty of them. But not one of those beauties had made him want to stare. Just stare.

He sighed and returned her phone to her. He noticed that her cutlery was arranged in a way that indicated she was done eating her lunch.

"Aren't you finishing your food?" he asked, gesturing to her more-than-half-full plate.

"I've had enough."

He gave her a questioning frown. Somehow he doubted it. She'd admitted she was hungry when she was deciding what to eat.

"Actually, I didn't like it much," she said.

He inhaled deeply, embarrassed. He should have taken her someplace else.

"I owe you dinner then," he said.

Jade's brows rose.

"I'm sure I can find a better place to take you next time," he said.

"Okay. Sounds great," Jade said, smiling prettily.

Damn, he was itching to kiss her.

"I have to go back to work," she said, checking her watch.

"Must you?" he asked, only half joking. Time seemed to have flown. He would have liked to hang around with Jade for a bit longer.

She gave him a disappointed nod as she got up from her seat.

He smiled, following her. At least he wasn't the only one sorry that this lunch was over—even if the food had left a lot to be desired.

They walked in companionable silence to the Bilton Machineries building while he carried Jade's big flower box. He wished he was holding her hand instead.

What? Hold her hand? Had he gone weird or what?

He smirked at himself, shaking his head surreptitiously. Whatever was happening to him, it was all

41

Jade's doing. And he wasn't sure yet whether he welcomed it or not.

He had to admit, though, it made him feel good all over.

He suppressed a snort. God, he needed to have his head examined. Maybe all this free time he'd had lately had turned his brain into mush. Or perhaps it was the effect of hanging around too much in his mother's flower shop.

Sooner than he'd wanted, they arrived at Jade's office building.

"Don't bump into anything now," he said as he handed Jade the huge bouquet of flowers.

She giggled. "I should ask your mum not to make them so big."

"Are you sure you don't need to cover that logo?"

"Positive. Mr. Bilton won't see it at all. He's away from the office all day. And I want the guys at work to see Ruby's logo when we present this to the birthday girl later."

He smiled. "Thanks."

"No. Thank *you* for walking again with me. I'm lucky you were at the shop today."

"We seem to have made it a habit to meet there," he said with a grin.

"I know," she said shyly. "Well, have fun in Belgium and good luck with the race. I guess I'll see you again when you get back."

"Yep. I'm back in two weeks." He kissed her goodbye on the cheek—another habit he seemed to have developed—and sauntered out of the Bilton Machineries building, feeling more bereft with each step he took away from Jade.

He guessed in terms of being physically attracted to a woman, he had it bad. It didn't help that Jade responded to his attention. It was cute how a woman in her midtwenties could still blush over simple words and charming smiles. He bet it would be more fun if he turned on his naughty streak around her.

He was starting to revisit his decision not to seduce her. After all, it wasn't her fault that she was Thomas Bilton's PA. As long as she wasn't complicit in Thomas' schemes, why should that be a problem? In fact, he could see the upside to it. Jade could be his source of information regarding Thomas' plans involving him and his mother.

As long as he and Jade were both fine with what he had in mind, why should he let his issues with Thomas get in the way? This was about him and Jade, not him and Thomas, right?

He mulled that thought while he walked back to Ruby's shop.

By the time he got there, his mind was clear. He wanted Jade in his bed more than he wanted to avoid her because of who she worked for.

Frankly, it wasn't really a matter of choice. Jade's pull was simply too strong.

With a bemused shake of his head, he went into his mother's shop. "I'm back," he announced to Ruby.

"Hello, darling," Ruby said as she fiddled with a new bouquet. "Rick called. He wants you to call him back."

"Thanks," he said, heading to a corner table where he'd left his phone to charge.

"I asked him to convince Jade to go to Greg's party with him."

Lucas whirled around to gape at his mother.

"He said he'll make sure of it," Ruby continued.

"That's what he said?" he asked with raised brows.

"Yes. At first he sounded like he didn't know what I was talking about. I think he was fully expecting that Jade was already going and was surprised that she hasn't made up her mind."

Lucas hid his grin. He could count on Rick to read the situation and act accordingly.

"So are those two dating?"

He snorted. "You know that Rick's not the dating kind, Mum. They're just friends."

"Good," Ruby said. "Jade doesn't strike me as someone who's into the fun-and-games-only relationships that you and Rick prefer."

"No," he agreed.

"I wonder if I'll ever know what's it's like to have a daughter-in-law?" Ruby said with a big sigh.

He laughed.

Ruby would be relieved if he found himself a proper girlfriend. Every so often, his mother would express concern that her past with Thomas was the reason Lucas shied away from relationships.

Lucas guessed there was some truth to that. His own father abandoning both him and his mother, and pretending they didn't exist, were hardly the stuff that inspired belief in love and happy endings.

But Ruby didn't have anything to feel guilty about. She hadn't done anything wrong, and Lucas was fine with his chosen lifestyle.

"Remember what you told me before?" Ruby asked. "You said that the time *I* decide to get married is the time you'll think about settling down. Well, it took me decades to stumble upon my soulmate, but I'm engaged now, am I not?"

"I *have* thought about settling down, Mum," he said.

Ruby spun to face him, her eyes round. "You have?"

"Yes. And the answer is no."

Ruby rolled her eyes, and he chuckled.

Dante, his mother's fiancé, was a man who'd popped into her shop to ask for directions. Getting engaged to him was another one of the reasons why Ruby had become quite vocal in her desire for Lucas to find 'happiness' with a special someone.

"So is Dante still on track with moving here in December?" he asked, hoping to change the topic.

"Yes, although that's not soon enough," Ruby said with a sigh.

Lucas smiled. Even though he'd questioned Dante's sincerity and motivation in proposing to his mother after only three months of dating, he now approved of his future stepfather. He'd never seen his mother happier. Unfortunately, Dante still lived in Brisbane and was waiting to finish a work contract before he could finally move to Sydney to be with Ruby.

"You know, darling, maybe you should try sticking with the same woman long enough. You move from one to another so quickly that you don't give yourself time to develop feelings for anyone."

"That's the way I like it." His heart thumped as if it didn't agree with that sentiment, just as Jade's face flashed in his mind. He frowned. What was that about?

"Oh well, I have hope for you yet," Ruby said. "We do have a family history of shunning relationships—and then when the right person comes along, love happens in an instant," Ruby said, snapping her fingers. "It happened to me. It also happened to your Uncle Syd and your Aunt Maria. We'd given up on love, then one day, bang! We're right in it. I have a feeling the same will happen to you, Lucas, only much sooner than you think."

"Sure, Mum," he said sarcastically. "I'm going outside to call Rick."

With some relief, he dialled Rick's number. It was a good excuse to avoid the topic that, frankly, scared the hell out of him.

"Hey, bro. So I'm supposed to take Jade Whoever-She-Is to Greg's party, huh?" Rick asked.

"Sorry about that and thanks for going with the flow," he answered. "No, you're not taking Jade Tully to Greg's party. She won't be coming. It was just an excuse we had to make up. My mum thinks you were just surprised to learn that Jade hasn't decided yet whether to go with you or not."

"So who is she?"

"It's a long story. I'll tell you when I come back in a couple of weeks."

"Interesting. Anyway, I called earlier to say have a good time in Belgium."

"Thanks. And if you happen to talk to Mum again—Oh, shit."

"What?" Rick asked.

"Mum's probably going to ask Jade if she's spoken to you. Damn." He raked his hair. This had become unwieldy. Somehow he had to warn Jade.

"What's it all about?" Rick demanded.

He sighed. "Could you come and meet me at the pub next door to the Bilton Machineries building at five this afternoon?"

"Bilton Machineries building?" Rick asked with obvious surprise.

"Yes. I told you it's a long story."

"I'll be there."

"Thanks, buddy."

Lucas hung up, rubbing his face. What an incredibly frustrating turn of events!

But he felt something else too.

Excitement.

He was going to see Jade again. Much sooner than he'd thought. Great.

CHAPTER FIVE

Jade stepped out of the building, still smiling from one of her officemates' comment that she had a hot boyfriend. Apparently, her colleague had seen Lucas walk her to the office earlier. Unfortunately, she'd had to set the record straight that she and Lucas weren't together.

Ahh, Lucas. When would she see him again? She was already looking forward to the dinner he'd promised.

She hadn't expected to have coffee with him last week, much less have lunch with him today, but she was certainly thrilled. She wouldn't go so far as calling them dates, but things were looking promising.

In her eyes, Lucas was the perfect boyfriend material. Seeing how much he cared about his mother boosted his desirability factor multiple times.

Was he already taken? He didn't seem to be, considering how he'd been flirting with her. Surprising that he was still available, but it appeared to be the case.

Would Ruby approve of her as a potential girlfriend for her son? And if she did, would Ruby be willing to play Cupid?

Ooh. That was an appealing thought. Maybe she could—

"Jade!"

Her heart skipped. There was Lucas, coming towards her from the pub next door.

"Hi," he said, rushing to her.

"Hi," she responded, aware that her faced sported a wide grin—probably too wide to be cool but darn, she couldn't help it.

"Do you have time for a drink with me?" Lucas asked.

Her smile widened. "Sure, I have time for a drink." Heck, she'd have dinner with him if he asked.

"Great."

Lucas briefly placed his hand on the small of her back to guide her to the pub, but that two-second touch was enough to make her nerve endings tingle.

"My friend Rick is in there too, waiting for us," he said.

"Rick? The one who's supposed to have invited me to Greg Carmichael's party?"

"Uh-huh. I left my phone at the shop to charge when I helped you carry that big bunch. Rick rang and Mum spoke with him. She asked Rick to encourage you to go to the party."

"Oh, no." And here she was thinking Lucas just wanted to see her. How disappointing.

"Yeah," Lucas said with a sigh, escorting her to a table where a man was grinning at them.

"Hello, Jade." The guy who was obviously Rick greeted her with a kiss on the cheek and a quick hug as if they were already friends.

"Hi, Rick. Good to meet you," she responded, warming immediately to the man.

"So I'm taking you to Greg's party, hey?"

"I don't think so," she said with a laugh, glancing at Lucas.

"No, he's not taking you to the party," Lucas answered with a comforting smile as he pulled out a chair for her.

She murmured her thanks and looked expectantly at the two gorgeous men.

"What would you like, Jade?" Lucas asked.

"Just orange juice, please."

"No alcohol?"

"Not today, thanks." Truth was, she was starving. Alcohol had always gone straight to her head at the best of times. Better avoid the risk of making a fool of herself.

"Anything to munch on? I heard they make mean Buffalo wings here. I've got to try those."

"Their Buffalo wings are to die for," she confirmed, her mouth salivating. "Their sweet potato chips are good, too."

"Coming right up," Lucas said with a wink before turning to Rick to get his order.

"Whatever you're having, bro," Rick said. "And an extra serving of the wings."

"I'll be back soon. Behave while I'm gone," Lucas said with a pointed look at Rick.

Rick smirked and an unspoken message passed between the two.

"So, Jade. You're a friend of Ruby's?" Rick asked when Lucas had gone.

"Yes. I've been a loyal customer for more than four months now. Occasionally, I hang around her shop and have coffee with her when she's not inundated."

"Did you meet Lucas there?"

50

"No. Hasn't he told you how we met?"

"Not yet. I just got here myself and we haven't had the chance to talk. All I know is that his mum is keen for me to convince you to go to my cousin Greg's party. Ruby seems to think you and I know each other."

"We're supposed to. But I'll let Lucas tell you the story."

"I have a feeling this has something to do with Thomas Bilton. Otherwise Lucas wouldn't be so stressed about it, and we wouldn't be meeting right next to the Bilton Machineries building."

"Yes. I'm Mr. Bilton's new PA."

"Oh, are you?" Rick asked, his eyes rounding. "And I suppose your boss has asked you to contact Lucas?"

"Yes."

"And that's how you two met?"

"Yes," she said reluctantly, hoping she wasn't divulging something Lucas didn't intend to tell Rick.

"Interesting," Rick mused, his curiosity evident in the way he was staring at her.

"Why do you say that?" she asked.

"Because Lucas has refused to entertain any request from Bilton or his people in the past. You must have had some effect on Lucas for him to have agreed to see you."

She chuckled dryly. "I'm sure Lucas would tell you how he got roped into meeting with me."

"I'm dying of curiosity."

"You and me both! I don't know anything about the conflict or whatever it is that's going on between Mr.

Bilton and Lucas, even though I seem to be right in the thick of it."

"You don't know anything?"

"No." She scrunched her face to show her disappointment at the fact.

"Well, we'll see what we can get out of him tonight then."

She nodded, trying not to look too eager. "If you asked, he'd tell you, wouldn't he? I haven't had much luck in that department."

"Haven't you? I'm sure Lucas would tell you anything if you ask him nicely," Rick said, grinning.

"I've already tried."

"I'd say you just haven't tried hard enough. Just keep batting your eyelashes at him and he'll eventually give."

She reddened. Darn it. Was it obvious to Rick that she was crushing on Lucas?

"I see Rick has been misbehaving," Lucas said dryly, coming back with their drinks.

"Hey, I wasn't," Rick said. "I was just telling Jade she's the kind of woman who could inveigle information from you."

"If she keeps on looking so cute blushing like that, I just might tell her what she wants to know," Lucas said, winking at her before clinking glasses with them.

"Well, I'm still blushing. So spill away, Mr. Renner," she said lightly even as her flush deepened.

"First things first," Lucas said. "My mum will no doubt ask if you've decided to go to Greg's party the next time you see her. We three should have the same story about why you can't go."

"I think first things first is why we need to lie to your mum, Lucas," she said softly.

Lucas ran his hand through his hair. Then he took a couple of gulps of beer, looked at Rick, then sighed. He was obviously reluctant.

"If you don't want to tell me, then it's okay," she said. "But I didn't mention before that Mr. Bilton has promised to let me know some details. I think you should know that."

Lucas narrowed his eyes. "He has, has he? Why would he do that?"

"Because he wants me to keep trying to get you to talk to him."

He pursed his lips and was quiet for a moment. "I don't trust that Thomas will tell you the whole truth, Jade."

"Then why don't you tell me the whole truth?"

He shook his head. "No offence, but it's not for anyone but the people involved to know. I'll make a deal with you, though. If you tell me what Thomas discloses to you about me and my mother, I'll tell you what I know."

She looked at him with dismay. "That might be a problem, Lucas. I happen to want to keep my job. Talking to someone else about confidential information could jeopardise it—even if the involved party is you."

"Then tell him you'll be talking to me about it. See what he says."

"Hm. Okay. If Mr. Bilton doesn't have a problem with that, then we have a deal."

"Great," Lucas said, offering his hand for a shake.

She took it, electricity zapping her from his touch.

"So when do you speak with Thomas?"

"He said he's waiting on a few things, then he'll let me know."

"Do you think it would happen between now and when I get back from Belgium?"

"I don't know. I'll remind him."

Lucas nodded.

"Lucas, do you think my working for Mr. Bilton will affect my friendship with your mum? Will I be forced to stop buying flowers from her?"

"Hey, don't worry about that. I don't see why this should affect your friendship."

"But I can't even tell her where I really work!"

"Jade, even *I* don't tell her everything. But if she ever finds out, I'll take the blame. I'm one hundred percent certain she'll understand. Also, you don't need to lie about what you do or who your friends are at work and all that. The only things you have to change in your conversations are the name of your boss and the company you work for. The rest could be facts."

She sighed.

"Hey, I have an idea," Rick piped in. "Why don't I take Jade to Greg's party? At least then she'd get to know some people and would have other things to talk to your mum about."

"No," Jade said, horrified at the thought. "That would complicate things further."

"I don't think so," Rick said. "No one there would raise an eyebrow at me bringing a woman they've never met. I have a big circle of friends, and they don't all mingle with each other."

"They'll just be surprised that you're bringing a date," Lucas said with a snicker.

Rick grinned. "So? You know I like shocking people. But I really think it will be easier for Jade if she met some of our friends. Then she'll have something to talk to Ruby about without having to make up stories all the time."

Jade glanced at Lucas. He seemed to be considering it.

"It would be too complicated," she insisted, telling him with her expression she wouldn't go for it.

"I actually think it's a good idea," Lucas said.

"Are you kidding me?" she asked.

"No. The Biltons and the Carmichaels know each other but they don't socialise together. My mum would be very pleased if you do go. She'd have much more fun at the party if you're there."

"And," Rick said, leaning closer to her, "it's a party that will be held in Greg Carmichael's own backyard. Aren't you the least bit interested in seeing his house from the inside? And wouldn't you want to rub shoulders with some celebs who'd be around?"

Jade stared at the two men. This idea was way outside her comfort zone. But who would want to turn down an opportunity to go to a Carmichael party and meet some fabulous people? More importantly, why wouldn't she grab at the chance to spend some time with Ruby— who might just be the person to get her closer to Lucas?

Her gaze went to the man she'd developed an insane crush on in such a ridiculously short amount of time. His smile was encouraging and his gaze was warm. Her heart fluttered, and her mouth opened to say okay.

"Good!" Lucas said. "Mum will be so relieved to hear that. Now let's get our stories straight."

Time flew by for Jade as she enjoyed chatting with the two hunks over delectable Buffalo wings and sweet potato chips.

*

"I gotta go. I have a dinner meeting tonight," Rick announced. "I'll see you on Greg's birthday, Jade. I'll pick you up at six."

"You know what?" Lucas said to Jade. "I'm sure Mum would be more than happy to give you a lift to and from the party."

"Sounds great! If that's okay with you, Rick?" She'd much prefer going with Ruby than Rick.

"Sure. I'll still RSVP you as my plus one even if you don't arrive with me," Rick said as he got out of his chair. He leaned down to kiss her goodbye on the cheek, then clasped Lucas' shoulder before walking out.

Jade watched him leave, sorry that her evening with the guys was coming to an end.

"I'm still hungry," Lucas said, facing her fully. "Wanna continue our conversation over dinner someplace else? It's getting noisy here."

Her heart hammered in her chest. "Sure," she said.

"Any preference?"

"As long as it's not eggplant, I'll eat anything."

"What's wrong with eggplant?"

"I'm allergic to it. I get swollen lips."

Lucas' gaze dropped to her mouth. For a long breathless moment he stared at it.

Gosh, it was probably wishful thinking on her part, but he looked like he wanted to kiss her. Unbidden, she licked her lips. They were getting dry and she was having a hard time breathing.

Lucas let out a gushy breath. "Let's go?"

She nodded, forcing herself to act relaxed as she got up. "I need to go to the ladies' first."

"Sure. I'll wait for you outside."

Jade pulled out her phone and called Cassie.

"I won't be home for dinner tonight, Cass."

"Oh, won't you? I was just talking to Lexie. She wants to have a girls' night in tonight. Erin wants to cook, so we're doing it at their place. Lexie said she went to your desk but didn't find you there. And you weren't picking up your phone."

"I'm not in the office anymore. I'm going to have dinner with someone. You'll never guess who."

"Who?"

"Lucas Renner."

"No way! How did that happen?"

"I'll tell you all about it later. But we just had drinks at the pub with one of his friends. Then he asked if I wanted to continue our conversation over dinner."

"Wow. That's exciting. Well, don't come home regretting that you've held yourself back again," Cassie said. "Get some more alcohol in you, then flirt, flirt, flirt without worrying if he'll respond back in kind. I dare you to."

"I'll try, Cass," she said, nervous excitement stirring in her tummy.

"That's not the answer I'm looking for, Jade. When you say 'I'll try' you know you're giving yourself an excuse to fail."

Jade sighed. Cassie had a point. How many times had she regretted being too cautious with men she liked? And how many times had she hoped for new opportunities to be bolder and fearless when it came to going for what she wanted?

Yes, tonight was the night she'd start shedding her old skin. The Jade who was fearful and insecure when it came to relationships belonged to the past. Tonight, she'd let her hair down and enjoy herself the way she'd always wanted.

"Okay. I'll flirt like there's no tomorrow."

CHAPTER SIX

Lucas stood outside the pub entrance, making sure he was hidden from the view of anyone coming out of the Bilton Machineries building or looking out of its windows. The last thing he wanted was for Thomas or his trusted henchmen to see him hanging around there.

He still regretted his actions of three months ago when, in a fit of anger, he'd called Thomas and told him to stop harassing his mother. And now, because of that rash decision, Thomas was galvanised into action. Lucas was sure that whatever Thomas was concocting, it was to counter the threat he'd made to Thomas. So now Ruby's reputation and well-being were on the line.

His gut twisted as memories of the first time he'd directly spoken to his biological father came rushing back…

*

Lucas took deep breaths while he was put on hold, waiting for the man he'd never spoken to all his life to answer his call.

"Thomas Bilton," came a bark.

"Mr. Bilton, this is Lucas Renner," he said in a steady voice. "I'm Ruby Renner's son."

"Yes? What can I do for you?"

Lucas smirked. While Thomas' words were accommodating, his tone was anything but.

"I don't want to take up too much of your time, Mr. Bilton. I just want to ask you to stop sending your people to bother my mother. I'm sure you've been told that I intercepted the last man you sent to intimidate her."

"What are you talking about?" Thomas asked.

Just as Lucas had expected, Thomas was denying it.

"Sir, I didn't call you to cause any trouble," he said with calmness he didn't feel. "I've read a certain news article recently, and I'm sure that spooked you. I guarantee you that my mother and I will continue to keep silent about your affair and her pregnancy thirty years ago. There's no need to scare and upset her."

"I don't know what you mean, Mr. Renner," Thomas said after a pause.

Lucas winced at the salutation. "Mr. Bilton, you can save your words," he said, anger creeping into his voice. "We both know the truth. But like I said, you don't have to worry. Both my mother and I will continue to hide the fact that I'm your son—"

"What? My son? Are you insane? You are not my son, Mr. Renner," Thomas said in a menacing tone. "So what is this really about? Did you call to scam me for money? If so, you've targeted the wrong person."

Lucas felt heat rise within him. He knew damn well why Thomas sounded so fucking confident. It was time to burst his bubble.

"I am not after your money, Mr. Bilton," he spat out. "I just want you to leave Ruby Renner alone. But I see you like playing hardball. Well, you know what? You're

60

threatening the wrong person. I'm sure you thought my mother didn't have a copy of the paternity test you took. Guess what? She does. And I do, too. Now, I don't have any desire whatsoever to take it out of its hiding place, because I don't want to have anything to do with you. But if you don't stop sending your henchmen to keep on intimidating my mother, I'll happily pull it out for the world—and your wife's family—to see. You wouldn't want that, would you, Mr. Bilton? So I'll say this again. Leave. My. Mother. Alone."

He hung up, hoping the old man got the message. And praying his mum wouldn't know about this call. She'd be terribly distressed.

*

Lucas was startled by a hand on his arm, and found Jade smiling at him.

"Hey, you look so deep in thought there," she teased.

"Just thinking about something," he responded, his lips curving at the sight of her.

"Shall we go?"

"Yes," he answered, taking her hand and leading her away from the Bilton Machineries building. The thought of spending a few hours with Jade made him feel better already.

"Hey, isn't the International Motor Show on this week?" Jade asked.

"It is. Unfortunately, I'll have to miss it. It finishes on Sunday and I leave tomorrow."

"Do you want to go tonight? It's your only chance to see it."

"No. I'd rather have dinner with you."

Jade gave him a happy smile that made his heart beat faster. "I meant *we* could go, if you want."

His brows lifted. "You want to go?"

"Yeah. I've always gone with my brother Jerry. But he doesn't have time this year."

"Are you sure?"

Jade nodded eagerly.

He grinned. "Let's go then."

*

Lucas shook his head as Jade took a bite of her burger.

"What?" Jade asked.

"I wanted to take you to a nice restaurant tonight. Not to another food court," he said, gesturing to the busy Motor Show dining area.

"Well, then, you still owe me that dinner," she said with that sultry but bashful smile of hers.

"Yes, I do," he said with a grin, staring at her beautiful face. He couldn't remember anyone else giving him a smile with such potency. It was… compelling.

"Aren't you gonna finish your food?" Jade asked. "You want to have enough time to visit all the exhibits, don't you?"

He laughed. On the way here, he'd found out that the car of Jade's dreams was on display tonight—the latest top-of-the-line BMW sports coupe.

"I'm starting to think I've died and gone to heaven that my date tonight is as excited as I am to walk around and check out cars," he said.

Jade giggled. "Maybe I'm the one who's died and gone to heaven that my date tonight took me to the Motor Show to see my dream car."

"Well, we better eat fast so you can start ogling that BMW," he teased.

"And that's all I could ever do," she said with a theatrical sigh. "Alas, it can never be mine."

"You never know."

"Yeah, I might win Lotto," she said sarcastically. "Anyway, is there anything specific you'd like to see tonight?"

"No. I'd love to check 'em all out. I like seeing how the new models from different manufacturers compare. And I love chatting with the staff who man the exhibits. I ask them curly questions to see if they know their stuff or if they're just full of bull."

"Oh, I'd love to see you do that. We better hurry then. We don't have much time."

Lucas grinned. Yes, he *had* died and gone to heaven.

*****

Lucas followed Jade to her door. She was so cute when she invited him up. She'd seemed almost embarrassed, but she'd quickly recovered and had smiled in that captivating way of hers.

He didn't want the night to end yet. He was enjoying every minute of his time with Jade. And frankly, he was looking forward to ending up in bed with her.

Except that he hadn't told her yet about his Mr. Fuck King title. If this had been a 'normal' date for him, he would already have inserted it in their conversation by now.

The title served a great purpose. It never failed to get the 'serious' ones scurrying away without his having to explain that he was only interested in no-strings. He'd never had females accusing him of misleading conduct when they knew about that label.

But every time he tried to mention it to Jade, he had a hard time breathing and his gut churned. His body seemed to be rebelling at the idea of Jade knowing about it.

Well, maybe he didn't have to mention it at all.

It was a stupid, juvenile title anyway. Apart from one useful function, being Mr. Fuck King was meaningless to him. It had been fun trying to wrestle it away from Connor because of the friendly rivalry they'd had back when they were working together. That was all.

So why should Jade have to know about it? No point in that, was there?

His breathing eased, and he relaxed again.

He'd just find another way to let her know he didn't do relationships... some other time.

CHAPTER SEVEN

Jade's hand was clammy as she opened her door. She was proud of herself for keeping her poise, though. It had been ages since she'd invited a date to her place.

After they'd left the pub, she'd ordered herself to ignore her too-cautious, over-analytical side. And this was the result of not holding herself back. She was alone in her apartment with an incredibly sexy man.

Was Lucas wondering if she might be interested in sex with him tonight? She'd flirted enough all through their evening that she wouldn't be surprised—or offended—if he were thinking it.

But she'd never slept with a man on a first date. In fact, apart from the two guys she'd agreed to go to bed with years ago, she'd refused to have sex until… well, until her date had got so frustrated from waiting that he'd lost all interest.

Problem was, the more she liked someone, the more she tended to hold out. Her fear that the man might lose interest after sex kept her from relaxing and letting go. Sadly, the guys had always ended up thinking she was just stringing them along. One had even accused her of being frigid.

She couldn't help it. Her first two sexual partners, both of whom she'd been totally infatuated with, had dumped her after just one night. The second one had even promptly cheated on her with a girl she'd considered a friend. When confronted, he'd said they just weren't compatible in bed. Devastating.

She knew it was her irrational fear of the same thing happening again that stopped her from moving forward with men she liked. But damn it, she was ready to burst past that relationship-destroying anxiety with the right guy. She'd been waiting for the opportunity. Unfortunately, the 'right man' didn't turn up in her life every day.

But here was one with her tonight. Lucas truly piqued her interest and, surprisingly, got her libido stirring readily. While she hadn't known him long, she felt comfortable with him already.

She so didn't want to muck up this chance to get to know him better—including physically. Except that she wasn't sure what she should do now that they were standing in the middle of her living room.

"Nice place," Lucas commented.

"Thanks. So do you want coffee or tea? Or wine, perhaps? I think we have a bottle of white in the fridge."

"Did you say *we*?"

"Yes. One of my best friends, Cassandra, lives here too. But she's with the other girls tonight and probably won't be home at all."

"That's good to know," Lucas said with a lopsided grin.

She blushed. Great. Now Lucas must surely think she was after sex.

"When my best friends and I get together at one of our places on a Friday or Saturday, we tend to just sleep over. That's why I'm not expecting Cassie to come home from a girls' night in," she explained.

"Were you supposed to join them, then?"

"Tonight's girlie thing was unplanned. And you'd already asked me out to dinner when I found out," she said with a smile.

"Hope they didn't mind that I took you away from them."

"No. Not at all. So what would you like to drink?"

"Wine, please. But only if you'll have a glass with me."

"Sure."

Jade went to the kitchen, pressing her hand against her tummy and willing for the butterflies to settle. "Relax, Jade. And just go with the flow," she said under her breath.

*

"So which is your favourite country to visit?" Jade asked Lucas. She was so relaxed that she was sitting casually on the couch with one of her legs tucked under her as she faced him. Good thing she'd worn a flared skirt today.

"I have many favourites," he answered. "But nothing beats coming home to Australia. When my friend Connor quit the Formula One team, I couldn't understand his motivations. I wondered why he gave up the lifestyle of being able to travel the world doing work he loves. But I get it now. After almost seven years of touring, I'm kinda tired of all the travelling. I think I'm ready for a new challenge."

"Change is good," she said, watching Lucas top up their glasses. "I was devastated when I was told I was being retrenched from my old job. I worked there for four years and enjoyed it. But—"

Jade stopped herself just in time. She almost forgot that Lucas had something against her new boss.

"Is Bilton treating you good so far?" he asked casually.

She nodded, taking a sip.

"Glad to hear."

She smiled at him. "I can't really talk about my work with you, can I? Just like I can't be fully open with it to your mum?"

"Hey, just because Bilton and I have bad blood between us doesn't mean I'm against his employees," Lucas said with a grin, playfully bumping his leg against her bent knee—and letting the connection linger.

"That's good to know," she said before taking a deep breath. That little contact was enough to make her breathing shallow.

Lucas stared at her and she felt her cheeks burn. She bet he could tell how he was affecting her.

"So it really doesn't bother you when we talk about my boss?" she babbled.

"Well, I would prefer that we don't talk about him," Lucas said.

"Of course."

"And what I'd really prefer to do right now is kiss you."

"Oh," she said, biting her lip to stop herself from smiling too widely. It would be embarrassing to be so uncool.

"What would you like to do now, Jade?" Lucas asked, his tone sensual as he ran a knuckle on her cheek.

"Maybe you should just kiss me to see if that's what I'd like to do or not," she said teasingly, hoping that sounded sexy.

His lips curved. "Great idea."

He took her glass from her and placed it on the table. Then he leaned over and kissed her. Slowly and sweetly. It was nice. Very nice.

"So do you like this?" Lucas murmured.

"Yes," she breathed.

"What about this?" His tongue swept across her bottom lip before it went inside her mouth.

She gasped, her arms snaking around his neck. Before she knew it she was lying on the couch with Lucas on top of her. And, geez, they were devouring each other's mouths.

They kissed for a long moment—she had no idea how long. But it must have been a good length of time as she was starting to feel discomfort with the way his body was pinning her. She tried to move her hips to find a better position. Lucas moaned and gave her some room by lifting himself off her without breaking the delicious contact of their lips. Gladly, she shifted, then felt Lucas pressing on her again... with him settled between her parted legs.

How the hell did that happen? She didn't mean to reposition them like this.

Or did she?

"Jade," Lucas said with a low moan, his lips travelling to her neck. Something hard ground against the apex between her legs. He was aroused.

But was she really ready for this?

"Lucas..." she said hesitantly, pushing against his chest.

He lifted his head to look at her.

"I just want you to know I don't do sex on the first date."

He inhaled sharply and gave her a patient smile. "Okay," he said and started to get up.

She curved her legs around his, stilling him. "I don't mind making out though," she said bravely.

Surprise flashed on his face before he groaned. "You're gonna drive me crazy, aren't you?"

"If you don't want to—"

She was silenced by Lucas' mouth back on hers, hot and seductive. Gosh, he really was an excellent kisser.

"How far can we go?" he asked as he kissed her throat.

"I don't know," she said truthfully. "I'll tell you when we get there."

He let out a low chuckle as he caressed her leg, increasing the friction between their hips.

She moaned, mindlessly arching against him.

"Am I allowed to do this?" Lucas ran his hand on the side of her body, then cupped a breast, kneading gently.

"Uh-hmm," was her response. But her clothes were in the way.

As if reading her mind, Lucas' fingers played with the top button of her blouse. "Can I undo these?"

"Yes," she heard herself answer, her heart pounding in her chest.

"You're beautiful, Jade," he said as he worked on her buttons. When he was done, he parted the material and his eyes roamed her chest. Her bra was the ordinary kind—she didn't have much need for sexy underwear— but Lucas seemed enthralled.

"Can I kiss you here?" he asked hoarsely, running a finger on the deep valley between her breasts.

"Yes," she said without much thought. *Most definitely, yes.*

With a low groan Lucas started raining kisses on her neck, then down to the exposed skin of her chest. He was unhurried yet insistent.

His fingers traced the upper edge of her bra as his erection rubbed against her mound. She didn't need to check to know that her panties were soaked. Goodness. No one had aroused her this quickly before.

"Let me see you," Lucas whispered, tentatively pushing her bra cup while looking at her for permission.

She nodded, on the brink of mindlessness. Just exactly how much of this did she think she could handle? She had no freaking clue. All she knew was she didn't want to say no.

Gently, Lucas pushed her shirt and bra straps down her shoulders. She lifted herself a little to help him bring them down far enough so he could move the cups and bare her breasts before his eyes.

"Jade," he said with wonder, staring before dropping his head back down to kiss her creamy skin.

He paid attention to every exposed inch, kneading as he kissed and laved.

But he avoided her nipples. They were hard and sensitised, crying for his attention. What a tease he was.

"Lucas," she cried, arching her back.

He grunted and went back to kissing her neck and face. Then he went on all fours above her, breaking the intimate contacts and leaving her bereft.

"Lucas." She heard the plea in her voice.

He reared to look at her face. Now even his mouth was no longer on her!

"I don't want to stop yet," she whispered.

Lucas let out a gushing breath, his gaze going to her erect peaks. He was breathing through his mouth, his tongue poking out.

"You can kiss them," she said shyly.

Lucas buried his head in the crook of her neck. She could sense how much he was trying to control himself.

"I want you to," she murmured, much bolder and more certain.

"I can't go any further without reaching the point of no return, baby," he said softly, still not moving.

"Then let's go past that point together."

"What?" he asked, staring at her in surprise.

"I want you."

"But you said…"

"I've changed my mind."

"No, Jade," he said, sitting up. "You just got too horny. We shouldn't continue. You said earlier you don't do sex on the first date."

She smiled. How sweet and gentlemanly. It made her want him more. "I told you I changed my mind.

Besides, haven't we had coffee and lunch on two occasions already? I'd say we can consider those as dates."

He gulped, then shook his head. But his breathing was still laboured and his eyes were trained to her chest.

"Can you just… um… kiss them before we stop?" Her face burned at her request, but she was finding some kind of liberation with Lucas.

"I already did," he said weakly.

"I meant my nipples," she said. Wow. She'd never been this forward before.

Lucas rubbed his face as if pained. When he looked at her again, his eyes were blazing.

He lay back on top of her, settling his hips once again between her legs. Ooh, the bulge in his pants was definitely harder.

"So you want me to lick these?" he asked, his seductive demeanour returning as he thumbed her hardened buds.

She gasped her answer as pleasure and desire raced in her veins.

Lucas rolled his hips against hers a couple of times, making her moan unashamedly. Then he bent down to lave a bud with his tongue while his fingers continued to play with its twin.

Oh, God. She was going to have sex on the first date after all.

She was tugging at Lucas' shirt when the intercom buzzer rang in a staccato kind of way. She froze.

"You expecting someone?" Lucas asked.

"No. But that would be my brother. They probably had dinner with his in-laws, who live in the next street. I better get that in case it's an emergency."

Lucas climbed off her and she trotted to the intercom, hurriedly fixing her bra and buttoning up her blouse.

"Hey, Jerry," she said.

"Hey. You sound breathless. Did I make you run?"

She blushed. Luckily, her brother couldn't see. "I'm fine. Is everything okay?"

"Yeah. We're on our way home from dinner at Mila's parents', but we thought you might want to see Mickey tonight. Can we come up?"

"Of course," she answered, looking down to check her outfit.

Lucas appeared by her side, an amused smile on his face. He fastened the last button of her top, which she'd missed.

"Jade?" Jerry said.

"Yeah?"

"Are you going to buzz us in?"

"Oh, sorry." Gosh, she was well and truly flustered. She glanced at Lucas' clothes to make sure he was decent before letting her family in the building.

"Do I look okay?" she asked Lucas, smoothing her skirt.

"You look perfectly fine. Especially with this you-caught-me-having-sex look."

"What?" She ran to the bathroom to check herself.

Lucas followed her, chuckling. "You look fine, Jade."

"If it ever comes up, don't you dare tell Jerry we were making out when he buzzed," she said to his reflection on the bathroom mirror.

"Making out? Heavy petting would be a more apt description, I'd say," he teased.

"Lucas!"

He laughed. "Do you have an overprotective brother? Should I climb out the window now?"

"No. It's just that… this is totally out of character for me." Truth was she was more worried that Jerry might be all over Lucas and scare *him* off.

For months now, Jerry had been pushing her to find a boyfriend. She knew her brother carried guilt that she might be putting her life on hold to help care for Mickey. Her having a boyfriend would alleviate some of Jerry's concerns.

There was a knock on the door.

"They're here. Sorry about this," she said.

Lucas caught her before she left the bathroom. "Relax," he said with a comforting smile, squeezing her arms.

She smiled and nodded.

*

"Hey, guys," she said, immediately holding her arms out for her nephew, who grinned cutely and went to her willingly.

"Is Cassie home?" Jerry asked as he and his wife Mila stepped inside.

"No. She's at Lexie and Erin's."

"Why aren't you with them?"

Jade didn't have to answer. Jerry had spotted Lucas.

"Jerry, Mila, this is my friend Lucas. He's Ruby's son—you know the lady who I buy flowers from?"

"Oh," Mila exclaimed. "Pleasure to meet you, Lucas. I love your mother's flowers."

"Thank you," Lucas said with a smile. "Mum has mentioned you love tiger lilies the best."

"I do!" Mila said, beaming.

Jerry held out his hand. "Hi, I'm Jerry. Great to meet you, Lucas. Sorry we turned up unannounced. We should have called first. But we won't stay long."

"Don't be silly, Jerry," Jade responded, smiling at her nephew. "I'm glad to see this little one tonight. Say hello to Lucas, Mickey." She held the baby's hand and waved to Lucas with it.

Lucas took Mickey's hand, pretending to shake it. "Hi, Mickey. Glad to meet you."

"What do you guys want to drink?" Jade asked Jerry and Mila.

"Nothing. We had a big dinner," Jerry answered.

"Have something, at least," Jade insisted, handing Mickey to Mila. "I'll make tea and coffee."

"Okay," Jerry and Mila said.

"I'll help you," Lucas said, following her to the kitchen.

She smiled at him. "You don't have to help."

"I want to," he whispered in her ear.

"Scared of my brother, are you?" she teased, getting cups from the cupboard.

Lucas chuckled. "Nah. I just want to do this." He cupped her face and gave her a sweet, lingering kiss.

She melted, snaking her arms around his neck.

She loved her family to death, but why did they have to turn up tonight of all nights? With a sigh, she placed her head on his shoulder.

"I had a wonderful time tonight," Lucas murmured, kissing her hair as he wrapped her in his arms.

"Me, too," she said, looking up at him.

They stared into each other's eyes, and Jade knew without a doubt she was falling for him. Fast. The kind of fall she wouldn't be able to stop even if she tried with all her might.

Mickey's loud cry broke the moment.

She sighed and reluctantly pulled away from him. "We better make these hot drinks."

"Okay. I'll watch you," Lucas said, standing behind her and putting his arms around her waist.

"I can't move," she said in half-hearted protest.

"What are you talking about? Your arms are free." Lucas ambled with her as she went to the sink to fill the kettle with water, his arms still firmly curved around her.

She giggled, not minding at all that Lucas' embrace was restricting her movements.

*

"I should go," Lucas said, checking the time.

"Oh, no, Lucas," Jerry said. "Please stay. We'll be on our way soon."

"I really have to go," Lucas said, rising from his seat. "I haven't packed yet and my flight leaves early tomorrow. It was great meeting you, guys."

Disappointment hit Jade but she didn't let it show. It was a shame Lucas couldn't stay.

She was aware of Jerry's and Mila's eyes on her as she walked Lucas to the door.

"See you in two weeks," Lucas said, giving her a kiss on the lips.

She forced a smile, not liking how far away two weeks were from now. "Have a good trip," she said. "And good luck with the race."

"Thanks. And hopefully we'll get to talk about what Thomas tells you in your meeting when I come back."

She nodded, feeling flat. He hadn't even gone yet and she already missed him.

Would things between her and Lucas still be like tonight in two weeks? She could only hope the moment hadn't passed.

CHAPTER EIGHT

Lucas took the unwanted coffee that Fely, Ruby's part-time assistant, insisted on making for him. "Thank you. You really didn't have to," he said.

"I wanted to," Fely purred, giving him the eye before heading to a customer and leaving him behind the counter.

He repressed his sigh. Fely had been angling for another date, even though he'd been clear from the beginning that there wasn't going to be a repeat of their one-night stand five months ago. Unfortunately, she was quite a determined woman.

When was his mother coming back from the errand she had to run?

He should have timed his visit to the shop better. But he didn't want to miss Jade when she turned up to get her flowers for Mila and Jerry. When her family had interrupted them two weeks ago, he'd totally forgotten to get her contact details. And he sure as hell wasn't going to call her at work. Thomas Bilton could overhear.

He'd been dying to know if Thomas had revealed anything to Jade yet. Would Jade talk to him about it? He hoped so. Even if she'd been told not to say anything, he'd still try to pry some information out of her. He couldn't not find out what kind of scheme Thomas was concocting involving him and his mother.

Apart from that, he simply couldn't wait to see Jade again, and resume what they'd started on her couch. He got hard every time he remembered how hot it had been. Jade's shyness just added to her sizzle.

He was glad they were interrupted though. In the heat of the moment, he'd forgotten to warn her about his no-strings policy.

Except that, once again, he was reluctant to do so. Why was that?

You damn well know you want to keep her, Lucas.

He let out a heavy, ragged sigh. In all honesty, he wasn't sure if he was ready for a relationship. It was something that never interested him in the past. Was he ready to give up his bachelor lifestyle, even though he hadn't been with anyone else since he met Jade?

He still didn't know the answer to that. All he knew was, right now, he wanted to be with Jade—and only her.

But it was okay if he didn't know what he wanted for the future yet, wasn't it? He and Jade had only just started going out. Surely she wasn't expecting anything serious at this point, either?

He snapped out of his musing when Fely walked towards the counter carrying a pre-prepared bunch of gerberas. She was followed by an elderly woman with the thickest makeup and pinkest lipstick he'd ever seen.

"Do you mind if I pay you with loose change?" the lady asked him.

"Not at all," he said cheerfully.

"Oh, thank you." The customer fumbled with the strings of a heavy-looking cloth pouch and emptied its contents on the counter.

Lucas scrambled to stop some of the coins from rolling off the table.

"I should have enough here, I think," the woman said. "Now, is this five cents or ten cents?" she asked, holding up a small silver coin and squinting at it.

"That's ten cents, ma'am," he said, trying not to grin too widely lest the lady thought he was laughing at her.

"Yes, I thought so. It might be faster if you helped me count."

"Sure," he said, starting to arrange the coins in order.

"You know, young man, my eyesight isn't perfect but I must say you're very good-looking."

He smiled. "Thank you. That's very kind of you to say."

"You're one lucky girl," the lady said to Fely.

"We're not together," Lucas said.

"You mean you're not a couple? Well, this could be my lucky day. What do you say, young man?" The elderly lady actually wagged her eyebrows at him.

Lucas smothered his laughter. "Aw, a beautiful woman like you would surely be taken already," he said.

"Eh," the customer said with a dismissive flick of her hand. "My husband can't get it up anymore. He said I could find myself a toyboy so I wouldn't be chasing him around the house. Anyway, we should probably stop this flirting and start counting. I have a bus to catch."

Lucas glanced at Fely, who was putting colourful wrapping and a ribbon around the stem of the bouquet. She was trying hard not to giggle.

He bit his lip to stop the chuckle that wanted to come out and focused on helping the spunky customer with her payment. He proceeded slowly, making sure the lady was keeping up with his counting.

Finally it was all settled and the customer left, looking very pleased with her purchase.

"She forgot to give you her address," Fely said when the woman was gone.

They burst out laughing and Fely was clearly overcome. She doubled over, clinging to him for support.

"I know I can rely on the two of you to man the shop while I'm gone," Ruby said with bemusement.

Lucas turned to his mother, only for his laughter to subside.

Jade was with Ruby, a hint of dismay evident on her face.

"I have a big rival for Lucas' affections, Ruby," Fely said through her giggles.

"Oh?" Ruby asked.

"A customer was here. You should have seen how she flirted with him."

"I see," Ruby murmured, although she looked confused.

"She was in her seventies, maybe eighties, with deteriorating eyesight," Lucas said dryly, his gaze focused on Jade. She looked uncomfortable.

A couple entered the shop. "Hi," said the woman. "Can we ask about your wedding packages?"

"Of course," Ruby replied. "Fely, could you put together Jade's bouquet, please," she said before escorting the couple to a small round table in one corner of the shop.

"What would you like in today's arrangement, Jade?" Fely asked.

Lucas watched as Jade gave her order.

God, he'd missed her.

Yes, he knew that already, but seeing her now made him realise just how much he'd *really* missed her.

He shook his head. Just how bad did he have it?

Fely went to the back room, presumably to get some supplies.

"Hi," he said to Jade.

Jade smiled at him. Thinly. "Hi."

"I was waiting for you."

"You probably want to find out if my boss and I have met about you-know-what, don't you?" she said in a low voice, casting a glance at Ruby.

"And have you?"

She nodded.

"That's good. But of course, that's only partly why I want to see you," he said with a smile. "Can I see you tonight? Maybe we can either go to your place or mine. We can have dinner first somewhere or order in."

Jade's gaze flickered to the back room door. He could read her face.

"You can't think that Fely and I are together, Jade," he said with censure. Surely she wasn't thinking he was trying to date two women at the same time.

Not that he'd generally cared about women thinking that in the past. The more they'd believed he wasn't after anything serious, the easier it had been to unlatch them from him.

But he did care about what Jade thought.

A smile spread to Jade's face. "Cassie will be home tonight. So maybe we go to yours?"

He grinned with glee. "My place then. I can pick you up after work outside of your building if you like."

"I have to drop by Jerry and Mila's to give them the flowers. How about I meet you wherever we're having dinner?"

He pulled his phone out. "What's your number? I can't believe that after all this time, I don't have it."

Jade told him.

"I'll text you my address. Come whenever you're ready."

"Okay, I'll let you know when I leave Jerry's," she said, her smile wider.

God, he wished he could lean over and kiss her. But his mother's shop wasn't exactly the place to do it with customers around.

"So how've you been?" he asked softly.

Jade opened her mouth to answer but stopped when Fely came out with an armful of blossoms.

"These flowers okay, Jade?" Fely asked.

"Yes, they look great. I think as long as there are at least three tiger lilies, my sister-in-law would be happy."

"I know Ruby gives you a discount. How much does she usually charge you?" Fely asked.

"Don't worry about this bunch," Lucas piped in. "It's complimentary."

"Why?" Jade asked, frowning.

"Mum's orders," he said, saying the first excuse that popped in his mind. He just felt funny letting Jade pay for flowers when he was behind the cash register.

"No. I'm paying for this, Lucas," she insisted.

"Well, I'm not taking your money. You can argue with Mum if you want to. But since she's with customers…"

"She's already too generous with her discounts every time I come here, Lucas. I can't accept this. She's running a business."

He shook his head stubbornly. He'd put his own money in the till to pay for Jade's flowers when she'd left.

"If she doesn't let me pay, I won't come back to order flowers from her again," Jade declared.

He stared at her. Yes, she looked like she meant what she'd said. Sighing, he held out his hand for her payment.

With a victorious smile, Jade handed him her credit card.

"How much does she usually charge you?" he asked dryly.

Jade told him. "And not a cent less," she added.

He rang up her purchase, not happy he lost this battle.

*****

Lucas swept a critical gaze at his dining table, making sure everything—including the candles—were in place, before running to answer the intercom.

"Hi, babe," he said, knowing it was Jade. "Come on up."

"Thanks," she responded.

Lucas took his chicken pasta bake out of the oven and placed it on the table before going to the door and opening it. He leaned against the frame while he waited for Jade to arrive.

He'd decided to cook tonight, since he had some time. Besides, this meant they'd have plenty of time to talk in private.

He was a bit nervous, though. He'd never cooked for a woman before. Well, in fact, he'd never had a date this 'proper' before.

He sighed, not knowing whether to be amused or worried by his unusual behaviour.

The elevator pinged and his heart thundered harder.

Ah, there she was, looking so beautiful with that incredible smile on her face.

"Hi," Jade said.

"Hi." He promptly cupped her face and kissed her lips. "I missed you," he found himself saying.

"I missed you, too," she breathed.

He placed his arm around her waist and led her inside.

"Something smells good," Jade commented, sniffing the air.

"I hope it tastes as good as it smells," he said with a laugh. "Ready to eat?"

"Yes, I'm starving."

He escorted her to the table and pulled out a chair for her.

"This looks nice, Lucas," Jade murmured, her eyes wide.

He merely smiled as he poured them some wine. He had no idea how to tell her he'd never done this before. And it scared him to think about that fact, so he pushed it away.

*

"This is really good!" Jade said.

"Thank you," Lucas said, relieved that his chicken pasta bake turned out perfect.

"So do you want to know what Mr. Bilton and I talked about?" Jade asked, peering at him through her lashes.

He smirked. "I was actually thinking we should do that after dinner. The topic might give us indigestion."

Jade laughed. "There's not much for me to say because he didn't tell me anything."

He frowned. "And what was his excuse for not telling you anything?"

"I said to him that I bumped into you at the pub when I was having drinks with a friend who turns out to be a buddy of yours, too."

"Rick, I presume?" he said with amusement.

"Yes," she said, sighing as if she was unhappy with herself—for lying to her boss, he supposed.

"Mr. Bilton got quite excited," Jade continued. "He asked if you avoided me or if you were friendly. I said that you were friendly enough for me to get the courage to ask why you got angry at his letter. Then I told him what we've agreed to—that you'll tell me your reasons if I share with you his reasons for wanting to communicate with you."

"Hope he didn't bite your head off after hearing that," he said, suddenly realising Jade's job security might be threatened. While he'd prefer her to be working somewhere else, he'd still wring Thomas' neck if the man sacked Jade because of this.

"Actually, he thanked me for having another breakthrough with you. He said he was more than happy to tell me what's really going on, but that he wants *you* to tell me first what it's all about. He said he didn't want to tell me anything that *you* wouldn't want me to know."

"What?"

"He made me sign a nondisclosure agreement that covers everything you and he tell me about this matter. I've already signed it and I have a copy of it for you in my handbag. He also recorded a message for you on my phone. I can play it after dinner."

"Okay."

He had no idea what was going on in Thomas' mind. But this new revelation was, once again, totally unexpected. He was more curious now than he'd ever been.

*

"Lucas, this is Thomas Bilton. I'm grateful that you're allowing Jade to help with our issue. As you know, she wants to know some details. I believe you've told her that you'll only speak about it if she tells you what I disclose to her. I presume this is because you're mindful of the agreement another individual has made with me in the past.

"I'm open to letting Jade know the details if it would help in resolving our differences. So I'll let you talk to Jade first. I'll follow your lead in terms of what you want her to know. All I want is to make right the wrong that has happened in the past.

Thank you, Lucas. I look forward to hearing from you."

Lucas slumped on his couch after listening to the recording on Jade's phone. Thomas' actions were becoming more and more unpredictable by the day. What on earth was the man up to? He rubbed his face, confused.

"Will I be remaining in the dark, Lucas?" Jade asked softly.

He looked at her, undecided.

"If it's too personal and you don't want to tell me, then can I ask a favour?"

"What's that?" he asked.

"Could you tell Mr. Bilton that you'd prefer for me to stop getting involved in this? It's just too hard being caught in the middle and not knowing anything. Mr. Bilton is my boss and your mother's my friend. And you're…"

The pinking of Jade's cheeks didn't escape Lucas. He smiled. She had no idea whether to call him her boyfriend. Well, he wasn't sure, either.

She was right about one thing, though. To continue to be dragged into this conflict wasn't fair to her if she knew nothing. Besides, he could tell Jade was sympathetic to Thomas' cause. He didn't want her thinking that he was the bad guy who simply didn't want to resolve an ongoing issue he was having with her boss.

"I suppose you should hear about it from me," he said.

"Thank you," Jade responded.

He took a sip of his wine before resting his head on the back of the couch. He stared at the ceiling as he decided where to begin.

CHAPTER NINE

"My mum and Thomas had an affair years ago," Lucas said after a long period of silence. "As luck would have it, I learned about it when I was sixteen."

Jade gaped at Lucas, stunned from his disclosure. He'd previously indicated that Ruby was involved in his conflict with Thomas, but she wasn't expecting this.

"Mum said she had no idea that Thomas was already engaged when they got together. He only confessed the day he said he wouldn't see her anymore. A few days after that, Thomas sent someone to make my mum promise never to divulge their affair to anyone. Obviously, Thomas was afraid that the truth would ruin him. Mum found out through an acquaintance that while Thomas had the Midas touch in business, it was his fiancée's parents—now his in-laws—who invested heavily in Bilton Machineries. It's not hard to come to the conclusion that if they'd learned about the affair, they would have pulled out their money. Bilton Machineries wouldn't be as big as it is now if that had happened." He paused, taking a sip from his wine glass.

"Mum said that the last thing she wanted was to see Thomas again after all that. But an unexpected situation forced her to contact him a few months after their affair had ended. Instead of responding to Mum's request to see him, Thomas sent someone else again. Mum was told to shut up and stay away from Thomas. They threatened to take away something very important to her if she continued to make contact with him. Mum made a decision then that it would be better for all concerned if she went along with what Thomas wanted.

"She probably shouldn't have caved. She had the perfect leverage to bring him down. But Mum didn't want to—or couldn't—deal with the pressure Thomas' henchman was putting on her. Even when family and friends encouraged her to take action, she refused, scared of what Thomas would take away from her if she did."

Lucas stared into space, finishing his wine.

"If I have my way, the world would know what a lowlife Thomas Bilton really is," he said. "But Mum made me promise to leave it alone. She said it wasn't worth messing with someone as influential as Bilton. I know there are ways to shame him and make him pay, but it would be at the cost of my mother's peace of mind. She doesn't deserve to relive her past hurts, especially now that she's doing well with her business and is happy with her life. So I also keep my mouth shut about their affair. Ironic how he's been wanting to communicate with me for the last few months.

"So that's why I've asked you not to let my mother know about Thomas wanting to talk to me, Jade, and why we have to maintain a fake story for her," Lucas said, his eyes imploring. "Heaven knows she's already been hurt enough by that man."

Jade nodded, empathising with him. But something did not fit.

"Lucas," she said gently, "do you think it's possible that Mr. Bilton is sorry for what he's done to your mum?"

Lucas snorted.

She placed a hand on his arm. "When he found out that you'd read the letter at the café, he was ecstatic. Then he had the same reaction when I told him I've spoken again with you. He was clearly very thankful. There was nothing about his actions that said his motives didn't come from the heart. And I'm not saying that because he's my boss, it's what I saw."

Lucas shook his head. "You misread his responses, Jade. I'm sure that his motivation is about protecting his and Bilton Machineries' reputations. I'm positive it's not about wanting to make amends for his past deeds. I can't see him having a change of heart for no reason."

She took a deep breath, not convinced. She might only have known her boss for a few weeks, but from what she'd seen so far of Thomas' conduct towards his employees and business partners, plus Lexie's constant praise despite his eccentric behaviour, Thomas seemed to be a decent, trustworthy man. "Mr. Bilton did say to me that he wants me to keep trying to get you to talk to him."

"I'm sure he couldn't stand the thought of not getting his way," Lucas said with a mirthless laugh.

"But don't you think he'd try to talk to Ruby? I'm surprised it's you he seems keen to smooth things with when it's Ruby he's hurt in the past."

Lucas stared at her long and hard before the look in his eyes changed. There was vulnerability there that made her want to comfort him.

"My mum's affair with Thomas happened thirty years ago, Jade," he said quietly. "She got pregnant."

Tears rushed to Jade's eyes. Now she knew the real heart of the matter. "Lucas," she whispered.

"Just three months ago he was still vehemently denying me as his son. Whatever plans Thomas has, it's not just to *smooth* things with me. He's feeling threatened because he's scared I'll let the secret out of the bag. He's countering that threat in an unexpected way. But I'm not fooled by his smokescreen."

Jade took a deep breath, not knowing what to say or think.

"Can you tell Thomas something for me?" he asked.

"Of course."

"Tell him I meant what I said—that I'm keeping my mouth shut as long as he leaves my mother and me alone. We're happy not to have anything to do with him."

"I'll tell him that. But I'm sure he'll have more messages for me to deliver to you if you continue to refuse to talk to him."

"I won't hold that against you," Lucas said with an attempted grin. "But please understand that I'll keep saying no to whatever your boss asks for. He's up to something, Jade. If I take the bait, it could mean trouble, especially for Mum."

Lucas tried to hide it, but Jade could see that his anger was his way of covering up his pain. Thomas' rejection had cut him very deeply.

Determination bubbled within her. She'd wanted out of this conflict between the two men, but now she was changing her mind. If there was anything she could do to straighten out some misunderstanding or heal some wounds, she'd do it. She wouldn't be able to do that if she was out of the loop.

"Jade."

"Yes?"

"Sit closer to me, please."

She scooted next to him and Lucas hugged her tightly, as if squeezing out whatever comfort he could.

She lifted her head to offer him her mouth. Lucas claimed it without hesitation, his kiss soft and seeking. She cupped his face and let her lips convey that she was there for him.

Her heart was bursting out of her chest. It felt as if it was too big, that half of it should be inside Lucas. The urge to meld with him, physically and emotionally, was almost overwhelming. She pressed herself against him.

Lucas groaned and deepened their kiss, raking her hair with his fingers.

Desire erupted within Jade. She locked her arms behind Lucas' neck and pulled him down on the couch with her.

At the edge of her consciousness, she sensed she was drowning. If she didn't swim for shore now, it would be too late. But she found herself not caring. Not while she was with Lucas.

Lucas reared up to look at her, his eyes dark with need.

"Bed?" he asked.

She nodded.

"All the way?"

She smiled, touched by his consideration. "If I say no?" she teased.

He grinned, gently brushing a stray strand off her face. "Then we're gonna have to continue with the game of seeing how far you want us to go," he murmured.

Ooh, she loved that game.

"It's a no for now then," she said, smothering her smile. "What first step do you have in mind?"

His lips curved sensually. "I think it's just fair that we pick up where we left off, don't you? If I remember correctly..." Lucas reached for the zipper at the back of her dress. "You were already half-naked."

She helped him take off her dress, happy with his suggestion.

"And this was already out of the way," he continued, unfastening her bra and discarding it as well.

She hadn't been *this* naked when they were interrupted the last time. But although there was still some shyness left in her, she was glad it wasn't enough to want to cover herself from his heated gaze.

"Now we restart," Lucas said seductively. Then he leaned down to capture her mouth.

"I think I remember my legs were around you like this," she said against his lips, parting her legs so he could settle in between, and wrapping them around his.

"You're right. And I was doing this," he said breathlessly, rocking his jean-clad hips against hers.

She gasped as she felt his burgeoning erection.

"Did you have enough of this last time, baby?" he asked, bending to lick a nipple.

Her answer was a little moan.

"Didn't think so." He kneaded one breast and tweaked the bud with his fingers while he gently sucked on the other.

She ran her fingers through his hair, breathing through her mouth, as she watched what he was doing to her. It made her hotter, seeing Lucas so enthusiastic while he stoked her desire. She tugged on his shirt, impatient to see him without clothes on.

He sat up to strip off his top.

Oh God, he was just as glorious as she'd imagined him to be. But instead of taking off his jeans like she'd expected, he leaned back down and started kissing her belly, then the side of her hip.

She quivered as he lifted her leg and placed it over his shoulder. He kissed the inside of her thigh, going higher and higher until he was nipping at the edge of her panties.

She bit her lip, this time from nerves. On the two previous occasions she'd had sex, only one guy had attempted to go down on her. When she'd told her date he didn't have to do it, she couldn't even tell who'd been more relieved—she or the guy.

"Lucas," she said, gently pushing his head away.

Lucas looked up, eyes round with surprise.

"Come back up here," she whispered.

"You don't like this?"

"Um… I don't know… but you don't have to—"

"You don't know?" he asked with a frown.

She gulped, embarrassment cloaking her.

Lucas smiled, placing a swift kiss on her thigh. "Can I just try, baby? You can always tell me to stop if you don't really like it."

She inhaled deeply and nodded. Hell, she'd been wondering for years why some people raved about oral sex—including her friends. Might as well try it since Lucas seemed agreeable to it.

He hooked his fingers on the band of her underwear. With some reluctance, she lifted her hips so he could slide it off her.

She closed her eyes, hoping she wouldn't involuntarily clamp her legs on Lucas' head if she turned out to be ticklish with this.

To her surprise, Lucas was back kissing her mouth. Did he just change his mind? She guessed she should be relieved. But frankly, she was more disappointed.

"You're so damn beautiful, Jade," he whispered as his mouth travelled to the sensitive area under her ear, then to her neck, and back to her breasts.

Her arousal, that had flagged momentarily, came roaring back when he played with her nipples again. Then his hand was between her legs, gently probing… teasing…

Fresh moisture rushed to the spot he was touching. Then his finger moved to her nub, coating it with her wetness. Ahh, this was definitely better than just her own fingers when she was alone.

"Do you like this?" Lucas asked, rubbing her deliciously.

"Yes," she moaned.

"Then I'm sure you'll like this, too," he said, travelling back down and pushing her legs further apart.

"Lucas!" she cried as he licked her. Damn. She didn't expect his tongue to feel so much better than his finger. Her friends were right. This was good. So good.

When Lucas closed his mouth on her sensitised clit and sucked lightly, her hips jerked.

"Do you like this, baby?" he asked seductively.

"Oh, God, yes," she gasped. "I officially like it."

He chuckled. "Then I guess you won't mind this, either." Lucas inserted a finger in her while his tongue flicked her clit.

Oh, fuck.

She surrendered herself to the sensations. Not that she had a choice to do otherwise. He was driving her crazy.

Soon, too soon, her orgasm loomed. She pushed his head to make him stop, not wanting this to be over yet.

"I thought you like this," he teased, refusing to obey.

"I do," she moaned, striving to stop her hips from grinding against his mouth.

"Come for me, honey," he coaxed, adding another finger inside her.

"It's too early," she complained.

"No, it's not. We're far from done, baby." He increased the pressure of his tongue on her clit, stroking her inner walls faster.

"Ahh!!" Wave after wave of pleasure engulfed her as she came hard, her body bucking off the couch.

When her body stopped contracting, she opened her eyes and found Lucas smiling at her.

"Hi," he said.

"Hi." She reached up to caress his cheek.

He kissed her softly on the lips. The taste of her body was on his mouth, making her blush. But, geez, even that was erotic.

"So beautiful," Lucas whispered as he proceeded to kiss and touch her all over again, making little moaning noises as his lips and hands roamed her body. Oh, he sure knew what he was doing. To her surprise and delight, she felt the stirring of another arousal.

"It's your turn," she said, reaching for the button of his jeans.

"Mmm," he responded, before getting up and lifting her in his arms.

"What are you doing?"

"Taking you to bed," he said with a grin. "You said you don't mind."

She giggled. "No, I don't."

Lucas had been so considerate that she wanted to give him back as much pleasure as he'd given her. But could she do that with her extremely limited sexual experience?

Hmm. Maybe she should ask him for tips on what would drive him wild.

CHAPTER TEN

Lucas kissed Jade's forehead as he walked to the bedroom with her in his arms. He was still buzzing from the high he got from making her come on the couch. Clearly, Jade hadn't had a lot of men—well, at least not a lot who knew how to pleasure a woman. He was thrilled he could give her an experience no one else before him had.

He'd never been this pleased with himself, which was a funny thing because he'd bedded more women than most guys he knew. But his satisfaction with Jade was greater than he'd felt with anyone else.

His desire for her was certainly strange—definitely something he wasn't used to. It wasn't only undeniable, it was also irresistible. Worse, Jade suddenly seemed… irreplaceable in terms of someone to satisfy his sexual needs. How weird was that?

While he was in Germany and Belgium, his work buddies had wondered what was wrong with him. He, Mr. Fuck King, didn't go home with a woman once in those weeks. He didn't even join his pals at the parties that usually guaranteed a stream of girls vying for the chance to stay the night with him. His friends had sworn he must be ill to have such uncharacteristic behaviour.

But all he'd thought of was Jade. For the life of him, he couldn't get her out of his head.

He wanted Jade. Desperately. So much so that he didn't want to scare her away with his usual no-strings talk.

He'd given up trying to figure out why his head was messed up. Right now, he'd rather spend his energy pleasing Jade in bed. It was less scary than wondering why she'd turned his world upside down.

He entered his darkened bedroom and Jade started kissing his neck.

"Hit the light switch, babe. It's right there," he said.

Jade did so, then went back to kissing him. Ahh.

He dropped her on the bed and climbed on top of her.

"Take this off," she said, trying to reach for his fly.

"You take it off," he murmured.

"Well, then, give me some room."

He grinned and kneeled on the bed.

Jade sat up, unzipping him and pulling down his jeans and boxer shorts to free his cock. It sprang up, hard and stiff. Hastily, he undressed completely and went back to his kneeling position.

Jade gaped at his length, her eyes wide. Then she closed her hand around it and explored.

He gasped. Her touch was tentative and soft. But damn, it made him burn even more. When she put the head in her mouth, he moaned her name.

"Is this good?" she asked in between gentle sucks.

He heard the uncertainty in her voice and it went straight to his heart. He was more convinced that her previous lovers had been selfish jerks who'd only focused on themselves, not even telling her how great she was.

"It's fucking good, baby," he said sincerely.

Encouraged, Jade tugged at the base while she continued to tease the head with her lips.

He threaded his fingers through her hair, flexing his hips ever so gently, making sure she wasn't uncomfortable.

"Mmm," Jade said, sounding like she was enjoying it.

"Your mouth feels good, Jade," he whispered. "So fucking good."

He let her continue for a while—or rather, he didn't have the will to stop her. But when Jade cupped his balls and enthusiastically took more of him in her mouth, he almost lost control.

He pulled away and hastened to get a condom from his bedside drawer. Jade watched him roll it on while running a caressing hand on his body. He smiled and gave her a kiss.

Jade lay on the bed and parted her legs.

He gawked at her. She looked so damn hot that he'd happily drive into her without further invitation.

But not yet. He needed her writhing with desire, soaked and begging for him, so she'd be ready for his size.

He kissed her lips, then travelled down to her amazing tits, knowing by now that Jade loved to have her nipples played with. Her moans told him she was building up again.

He moved further south to once again put his mouth to good use. She whimpered.

Soon her panting was faster and louder.

"Lucas," she cried.

"Yes, baby?"

"I'm supposed to be making you come," she said with a cute whine even as she held his head in place.

"You will," he said with certainty, then teased her entrance again with the tip of his tongue.

"You already have a condom on," she said, gasping.

"Uh-huh."

"I want you now."

"Mm. Don't you like this?"

"Yes, but…" Her hips undulated as she sought more friction with his mouth.

"But what, sweetheart?"

"Lucas, please fuck me," she said in the softest whisper.

He groaned. Other women had said that to him many times before. But coming from Jade, it was the sexiest thing he'd ever heard.

He crawled up on top of her. "Is this what you want?" He rubbed his erection on her nub.

"Yes," she cried, angling her hips for him.

"Ah, Jade," he said through gritted teeth as he pushed in slowly. God, he was only halfway in and he could already tell she was like heaven.

"Okay, baby?" he asked, straining not to move until she'd adjusted to him.

She smiled sweetly. "Yes. I want more."

Argh.

He moved slowly. Over and over.

"Lucas… Lucas…" Jade chanted.

"Feel good, baby?" he asked, unable to help but thrust faster.

"Yes," she gasped.

"What about this?" He thumbed her clit at the same time.

"Oh, God!" Jade cried, grabbing his behind and urging him to go deeper.

He was more than happy to comply, already losing control. The fire burning inside him was all-consuming.

Jade tensed, her legs squeezing him tight and her fingers digging on his shoulders.

He groaned, his hips pumping harder as his pleasure spiralled from watching Jade in the throes of climax.

She clutched him, calling his name out loud as she trembled violently from her orgasm.

"Jade… fuck!" he cried, erupting inside her with a force so great stars swam in his eyes.

*****

Lucas stirred when a faint melodic sound came from his living room. What the hell was that? It stopped before he could figure it out.

Beside him, Jade bolted to a sitting position on the bed, looking disoriented.

Wakefulness came and he grinned. He couldn't believe they'd fallen asleep.

"Hey, babe," he said, caressing her leg and sitting up to kiss her shoulder.

"What time is it?"

He checked the digital clock on his bedside table. "Two fifteen," he said in surprise just as the melodic sound started again.

"Oh, shit. That's my phone," Jade cried, jumping out of bed. She tried to pull the sheet to wrap herself with it, but it snagged around his legs. She abandoned her efforts and ran to the living room, naked.

Amused, he followed her, taking the blanket with him. He'd never dozed off with a woman in his bed without prior agreement. He and Jade must have been exhausted enough—and relaxed enough—to have zonked out without realising it.

"Hey, Cassie," Jade said to the caller.

In the silence of the room, Lucas could make out Jade's best friend exclaiming her worry. He sat on the sofa and pulled her to his lap, then he draped the sheet around them.

"Yes. I'm fine, Cass," Jade said, resting her head on his shoulder. "I'm at Lucas' and, um, we fell asleep... No... I'm sorry... I didn't plan to fall asleep... I know. I should have called earlier... Oh, God. Okay... Thanks, Cass. I'll talk to you when I get home. Bye."

"You got your friend worried," he said, squeezing her tight and placing a kiss on her hair.

"Not just Cassie. Also Jerry, Mila and the other girls, because Cassie called them when I didn't come home. I have to call Jerry," she said, dialling her brother's number.

Lucas heard Jerry's expletives. Jade tried to soothe him, apologising and explaining again that she'd fallen asleep in Lucas' apartment.

Jade sighed when she finished the call.

"Jerry okay?" he asked, lightly rubbing her back and arms.

"Yes. Just really mad because he'd thought I was lying unconscious in a ditch somewhere or got kidnapped or something."

"I'm sorry," he said, placing butterfly kisses on her face.

"It's not your fault. Oh, wait. It *is* your fault. You must have drugged me," she said with a grin. "We didn't even hear their earlier calls."

"Yes, I mixed my top secret pleasure potion with your food," he joked, standing up with her in his arms. "Let's go back to bed. I have more to give you."

*****

Lucas checked out the sports car Connor was souping up for Rick. For someone whose business was selling luxury cars, Rick wasn't content with factory-built vehicles.

"Looking good," he said with approval.

"Is this making you itch to get your hands on cars other than Formula One?" Connor asked.

"Yeah. I should just totally quit and join you, like we talked about."

"Really? You're ready to quit?" Rick asked.

"Getting there," he admitted.

"You do know you can't keep the title Mr. Fuck King if you're no longer travelling internationally and having girls in every country, right?" Connor teased.

He chortled. "Come on, dude. How many times do I have to tell you that my primary purpose of going after

107

that title was to wrestle it away from you? Done and dusted."

"Hey, you didn't wrestle it away from me," Connor said. "It passed on to you by default when I quit."

"Well, the fun's gone now that I don't have the likes of you to make a contest of it."

Connor chuckled. "Anyway, I heard it through the grape vine that you haven't been living up to your reputation in your recent trips."

He rolled his eyes. "Trust the guys to blab."

"So what's up with that?" Connor pressed. "That doesn't sound like you."

He shrugged. "I'm entitled to some off days, am I not? I was more concerned about putting my case up regarding cutting back on Formula One work," he added as an excuse.

"Hey, is Jade still coming to Greg's party this weekend?" Rick asked.

"Yep," he said, hoping the guys wouldn't ask too many questions about her. They were trying to keep it quiet.

"Who's Jade?" Connor asked.

"Bilton's PA," Lucas said wryly.

Connor stared at him. "*That* Jade? The one you said conned you into reading a letter from Bilton?"

He nodded.

"Why the hell is she going to Greg's party?"

Lucas told Connor about Jade's friendship with his mother.

"Wow. What are the chances, huh?" Connor said.

"I know."

"Have you Fuck-Kinged her yet?" Rick asked, his brows furrowed.

He laughed—a little weakly—and he neither confirmed nor denied.

Jade had been staying over at his place almost every night for the last two weeks. He just couldn't get enough, and he wanted to spend as much time with her as possible before he had to leave for work again. In all that time, he wouldn't have said he'd Fuck-Kinged her. It simply didn't sound right to use that term on Jade.

Rick and Connor stared at each other.

"Wait," Rick said. "Jade wouldn't have anything to do with you going all celibate in your trips, would she?"

"No," he lied.

"I've seen the way you looked at each other at the pub," Rick said suspiciously.

"So? I look at all women I'm attracted to like that. And she's not the first to make cow eyes at me."

"But has she agreed to sleep with you?" Rick asked.

"Hey, this is Mr. Fuck King you're talking about, Rick," Connor said. "What kind of question is that?"

"I've met Jade, and she's not the type to be interested in Lucas," Rick said.

"What do you mean she's not the type to be interested in me?" Lucas asked, affronted. Of course Jade was interested in him. She couldn't keep her hands off him.

"Isn't she the relationship-seeking type? I'd be surprised if she goes for you."

"She has, though. Gone for me, that is."

"Even after you told her of your relationship-repellant title?" Rick asked in surprise.

He stayed silent.

"You haven't told her?" Connor asked, brows raised. "Wow. What's happened, bro? Did you fall in love or something?"

Lucas' heart thundered even as he snorted. "Don't be ridiculous, Connor."

"So why have you changed your MO with Jade? Because of Bilton?"

"Yes," he uttered.

That was only a small part of the truth, of course. The real reason was he simply didn't want Jade to disappear from his life.

He'd been having the best sex with her. For him, she was simply the hottest woman on the planet.

But apart from that, Jade made him feel... happy. He just loved being with her.

So did that mean he was ready for a committed relationship? It still scared him that being in one would mean losing a heck of a lot of the freedom he had now. But hadn't he become disinterested in that kind of freedom anyway?

A couple of snickers pulled him out of his musing. Connor and Rick were staring at him, chuckling.

"What?" he asked.

"You look totally lost there, dude," Rick said.

He smiled, embarrassed.

"I reckon you should keep seeing this Jade woman," Connor said. "See where it leads. She seems to have this massive effect on you."

"But I've always maintained that if I have a choice between being an emotional slave of some woman or being free to do as I want whenever I want, I'd choose the latter any day of the week. Why would I want take a path to a destination I don't want to end up in?"

"Why are you in a conundrum about this if you already know what you want?" Connor challenged.

He didn't have an answer to that.

"Sometimes your heart will want to go where your head doesn't. It's just a question of which will win."

"Shouldn't I want my head to win?"

Connor grinned. "Sounds to me like your heart's being stubborn, dude."

He laughed, just as he remembered his mother's words.

'We've given up on love, then one day, bang! We're right in it. I have a feeling the same will happen to you, Lucas, only much sooner than you think.'

He sighed, smiling. Maybe his mother's prediction had come true.

"Um, I want to tell you something," Rick said.

"What?"

"You'll keep this confidential, right? I don't want my business to have a bad rep among any of my clients."

"Of course," Lucas said, frowning at Rick's tone.

"There's a policy in place at work where my staff needs to alert me when someone well-known buys a car. It's so I'm able to toss in some personal touch if warranted. Yesterday, someone ordered a top-of-the-line BMW coupe, latest model. The pay went through Thomas Bilton's credit card, but the ownership was for Jade Tully."

Lucas stared at Rick, his heart racing.

"Maybe he's just giving her a bonus, right?" Rick said. "I mean, Bilton Machineries has made the news before for being generous to their staff."

"Not that generous," Lucas murmured. "Could it be one of Bilton's company cars for his PA to drive?" he asked hopefully.

"No," Rick said. "The paperwork was for private ownership."

Lucas inhaled sharply, every cell in his body rebelling against the implications of Rick's revelation.

"I'd be careful around this Jade woman then if I were you, bro," Connor said quietly.

"Yes," he agreed, although his mind seemed incapable of coherent thought. Everything was in a jumble in his head.

"Hey, you're leaving again in a couple of days," Rick said gently. "You could recalibrate while you're in Japan."

"Good idea," he murmured, feeling a thick, dark cloak wrap around his heart.

CHAPTER ELEVEN

Jade sighed with impatience. Thomas Bilton was still on the phone, and his meeting with her should have started ten minutes ago.

He'd cancelled on her twice already in the last couple of weeks, saying he was waiting for some critical information he wanted to show her during their discussion. Strangely, Thomas hadn't even wanted to know yet what Lucas had said to her. Thomas' reason was that he didn't want her thinking he'd cheat and tailor his response based on what Lucas had disclosed. He wanted her to fully trust his words so she could convey his message to Lucas with confidence that he truly meant what he said.

That made some sense to Jade. But to Lucas, it was simply Thomas manipulating the situation again.

Maybe Lucas was right. Maybe Thomas' intentions weren't as honourable as she'd originally believed.

She buried her face in her hands. What could she do if that were the case? She needed this job. Her pay was above industry standards and the perks were fantastic. And she truly enjoyed the actual tasks and the people she worked with—even Thomas.

But in her heart she knew that she wouldn't be able to stay here if Lucas' suspicions proved correct. How could she continue to work for a man who intended to keep hurting people she cared about? Ruby was a good friend of hers, and Lucas was…

As far as she was concerned he was her boyfriend, even though it wasn't official. They'd agreed not to tell anyone that they were seeing each other, apart from trusted friends and family. Lucas worried about what Thomas might do with the knowledge.

Now she was worried too. After his initial enthusiasm about Lucas' willingness to open up to her, Thomas seemed to have retreated—or changed his mind about talking.

"Jade."

She lifted her head. Thomas was standing at his door and beckoned for her to come in. With a deep breath, she followed.

She took a seat and waited for Thomas to settle himself and speak first.

"The information I was hoping to get my hands on didn't materialise," Thomas said with a deep, displeased frown. "I'd been hoping to have it for this discussion."

Jade's heart sank. Was he postponing this meeting again?

"When you told me two weeks ago that Lucas had agreed to listen to my recording, I could tell from your face that he'd told you some pretty important facts, Jade."

She stared at him. Her poker face had failed her again, by the looks of it.

"First, may I remind you of the nondisclosure agreement you signed?"

"I remember, sir," she said, her breath catching from anticipation.

"Good. Now, I've said that I'll follow Lucas' lead on what you should know. I suppose we should begin with that. So what do you already know, Jade?"

"That you had an affair with Ruby Renner thirty years ago when you were already engaged to Mrs. Bilton, and that Lucas is your son," she said quietly.

Thomas nodded, inhaling deeply. "Now I'll tell you my side of the story."

"Okay," she whispered.

"I did have an affair with Ruby—a very brief one. It was during the time when Diana and I had a big argument and weren't talking to each other. I'm not proud of the fact that I went to the arms of another woman when I was angry with Diana. I'm also not proud of the fact that I let Ruby believe there could be something between us. My only excuse is that I was young, successful and terribly cocky, thinking I had the whole world at my feet and that I could get away with anything.

"I broke it off with Ruby when Diana found out about us. Diana left the country to be away from me. I realised then that I didn't want to lose Diana. I begged for her to take me back, and eventually she did—but that's an altogether different story.

"Diana's father was livid when he heard about my affair with Ruby. He said I wasn't worthy of his daughter or of the help he's given me to build my company. He'd invested heavily into Bilton Machineries, you see."

Jade nodded.

"I promised him that Ruby and I were well and truly finished and that I was totally committed to his daughter. But he wouldn't hear any of it and pulled out all the money he'd poured into Bilton Machineries. I couldn't really blame him."

Jade raised her eyebrows. Lucas didn't know about that.

"With severe cash flow problems from Diana's dad withdrawing his money, I was afraid that I wouldn't be able to keep the company afloat," Thomas continued. "I couldn't borrow any more from the banks. Fortunately I managed to sell my vision to a couple of other people, who agreed to invest in the company.

"I was trying to reconcile with Diana while all that was going on. She didn't know if she could trust me again. She was also afraid that Ruby might not be totally out of the picture. To try to alleviate Diana's concerns, I sent someone to ask Ruby to swear that we were over and that she would keep our affair a secret for Diana's sake. Ruby was angry enough to say that she didn't have a problem with that because she never wanted to see my face ever again."

Thomas slumped back on his chair, as if this was depleting his energy.

Sympathy welled up inside Jade. Thomas looked like he was reliving the suffering as if it were happening now.

"One day I got a message," Thomas said with his eyes shut. "It was from Ruby, wanting to talk to me about something extremely important. I didn't want to face her then. Diana and I were just rebuilding our relationship. So I sent the same assistant to find out what Ruby wanted. She said she was pregnant.

"I was in shock. I didn't want to believe her. She would have been about eight months along then and I wondered, if I was the real father, why she'd waited that long to tell me. I suspected that she wanted to blackmail me. At the time, my company was in the news because of several high-profile contracts with overseas partners.

"So once again I sent someone to see her, to tell her that we'd be doing a paternity test when the baby was born. I wanted to keep everything at arm's length because Diana didn't know anything about it at the time. I didn't want to have to tell Diana until I was sure I was the father of Ruby's baby.

"My assistant arranged for a private clinic to do the tests, making sure nondisclosure agreements were signed. The results said that I *wasn't* Lucas' father."

Jade gasped.

"I asked for my assistant to talk to Ruby and tell her once and for all to stop hassling me. I had proof—or I thought I had—that she'd lied. I've never heard from Ruby again after that.

"Then about four months ago, I received a phone call from Lucas. I was intrigued about why Ruby's son would be calling after all these years, so I picked up the call. Lucas accused me of sending someone to keep harassing his mother. I was angry and incredulous. The last time I sent someone to see Ruby was after the pregnancy test. I couldn't believe that her son would call me out of the blue and come up with something totally ridiculous and baseless after so many years.

"We exchanged angry words until Lucas brought up the paternity test. He said he'd pull it out for the world to see if I didn't leave Ruby alone. I was both laughing and

117

cursing when Lucas hung up. His claims were outrageous. But something in the way he spoke made me check my copy of the test. Of course what was shown in the paper hasn't changed miraculously. It still said that I wasn't Lucas' father. But something still niggled me, so I got in contact with the private clinic who did the tests and asked for another copy. That was when I found out that what I'd had in my hands for almost thirty years was a bogus report."

Jade was having trouble breathing. She couldn't believe what she was hearing.

Thomas blinked several times, his eyes watering.

"I was enraged. I threatened to sue the clinic, but their records show that they *did* send the correct reports to the concerned parties. That left my assistant, who'd handled the whole thing for me. Unfortunately he's dead. He passed away ten years ago.

"I don't know who else is involved in this or what their motivations are. But if someone is still visiting Ruby to this day, then someone is obviously keen on making sure this deception remains hidden. I'm still working on finding out who has kept me away from my son all these years, Jade. It's frustrating me that we're coming up with a blank. It would help if we could interview Ruby and Lucas, but I don't want to alienate them any further. I want Lucas' permission first before I make contact with Ruby."

Thomas ran his hands on his face. "This is a nightmare worse than anything I've ever imagined."

"Mr. Bilton," Jade whispered in sympathy, not knowing what else to say.

"I told Diana about this when I found out about the fake test result. She was in shock, as you can imagine.

118

But she's a good woman and is sympathetic to what's happening. I have her full support in trying to reconcile with Lucas. As you know, Diana and I were not blessed with children. That I actually have a son is an unexpected gift that I'm extremely grateful for. Unfortunately, he hates me and I can't say I blame him, even though I've been at the receiving end of this deception as well." Thomas covered his face with his hands, breathing deeply.

Jade pressed her fingers to the sides of her eyes, surreptitiously wiping away her tears. Her heart ached at Thomas' story, but she was also joyful for Lucas. His father hadn't rejected him after all.

"Please tell Lucas all this, Jade."

"I will, sir."

"Thank you," Thomas said, smiling at her. "I do believe Lucas has taken a shine to you. And you to him."

She blushed. There was no denying that.

"I'm glad. I do want to make amends for what I've put Ruby and Lucas through in all these years. Could you help me with something regarding that?"

"Of course, Mr. Bilton."

"I had a private investigator give me some information about Lucas and his mother when I was trying to sort out the fake paternity test. I didn't know anything about their lives since I haven't had any dealings with them in the last thirty years, so I just wanted to know some details. I don't think Lucas would appreciate knowing that at this point, though. So could you not tell him that bit until he's mellowed enough and agreed to talk to me?"

She nodded. She could already imagine Lucas blowing up if he learned that Thomas had had an investigator digging into his and Ruby's lives. It could be detrimental to the reconciliation process.

"I felt very proud when I found out that Lucas works as a mechanic for a winning Formula One team. We obviously share the same interest in machines, although mine are of the big, heavy, slow kind," Thomas said with a chuckle. "I imagine he must be very good at what he does. I like to tinker with cars, too. Anyway, I told him in the letter you handed to him that I would love for him to consider being part of Bilton Machineries. Whatever skills he's acquired would surely be transferable to what we do here. And while I plan to work until I'm no longer capable—hopefully for ten more years, at the very least—I don't want this company passing to the hands of just anyone when I'm gone. I don't have siblings, so I don't have any nieces or nephews. Diana has one brother who has a daughter, but they have no interest whatsoever in this business. But I believe this is right down Lucas' alley. My hope is that while I still have plenty of time, I could show him the ropes so he can be prepared to take over this company when I'm no longer capable."

"He doesn't feel any entitlement to Bilton Machineries, sir," she said. She was touched by what Thomas had said and didn't have the heart to tell him that Lucas didn't want anything to do with his company.

"I know," Thomas said with a sigh. "That speaks loudly of how much he is against me. The chasm I must cross before he'll accept me is wide. But you can help me start building that bridge, Jade, if you are willing."

"Of course, sir."

"Great. Diana has suggested a dinner at our house with the four of us. That way, Lucas can see that Diana welcomes him with open arms."

"I don't think he'd agree to that at this point, Mr. Bilton."

"Just try, Jade. Please. We have to keep chipping away. I'm not getting any younger. I don't want to waste any more time in getting to know my son," Thomas said with a wobble in his voice.

"Okay, sir."

"Thank you, Jade. I want you to know that I appreciate your help very much. And I do believe that you're the key to getting Lucas to open up to me."

She nodded. How she'd accomplish the task he'd just asked her to do, she had no clue.

*****

"It doesn't make sense," Lucas said, frowning.

"Which part doesn't?" Jade asked, looking at him with concern. She'd hoped that Lucas would greet her news with some relief, even joy. But all she could see on his face was stark scepticism.

"It's unbelievable that from my *one* phone call with him, he got in touch with the clinic to double check the paternity results. Then *suddenly*, not only does he want to play dad and son, he also wants to prepare me for a future takeover of his beloved company. He hardly knows me, Jade. What sane man would make snap decisions like that regarding a person he's never spoken a single word to until four months ago—son or not?"

121

"He is a bit eccentric," she said, looking around the restaurant to make sure no one could overhear their conversation. "Anyway, I believe him."

Lucas' scowl got deeper.

"I can see where you're coming from, Lucas. But I was right in front of Mr. Bilton when he told me his side of the story. His emotions are just as real as yours are right now. I really think he's telling the truth."

"And I still think he has ulterior motives," said Lucas, glaring at her. "You've known the man for, what, four months? How could you make that call when his actions for the last thirty years compared to these last few months say otherwise?"

She squeezed his arm, disliking that he was getting mad at her. "Maybe you should talk to him. Face to face. Then you can decide for yourself whether to believe him or not."

"Maybe," Lucas said, to her surprise. "I just want to drag the truth out of the man," he muttered.

She smiled, relieved with this progress. "He's invited us to his house for dinner with his wife," she said tentatively. "Maybe we can go when you come back from Japan?"

"What?" Lucas asked.

"He's told his wife Diana," she said gently. "And they both want to make you feel welcome in their home—and their lives."

Lucas continued to scowl at her, searching her face.

"You don't think it's a good idea?" she asked.

"Why are you pushing this so much, Jade?" he asked harshly. "I thought you understood perfectly well why I don't trust your boss. Why are you suddenly so insistent?"

"I just thought that since you've agreed to meet with him face to face…"

Lucas shook his head. "If you don't mind, I don't want to talk about this anymore."

She suppressed a sigh.

For the rest of the night, she tried to carry on light conversation. Lucas only responded with a word here and there. He was cold towards her and she felt it acutely.

*

"I'll drive you home," Lucas said as he started the car.

"I thought I was going to stay over at your place tonight."

"I haven't prepared for my trip to Japan yet. My flight leaves very early tomorrow," he said flatly.

"Okay." Her eyes watered but she forced herself to get a grip. Lucas was just upset and she could understand why.

When he stopped in front of her apartment building, she reached for his hand. "Please don't be mad at me."

Lucas gave her a small smile that didn't reach his eyes. "I think we should cool off, Jade."

She gaped at him, unable to believe what he'd just said. "Lucas… Why?"

Lucas stared out the window, his expression unreadable.

She waited, aware that her heart wanted to jump out of her chest and cling to him.

"There's something I should have told you from the beginning," Lucas said quietly, still not looking at her. "I'm not after a relationship, Jade. I never have been. I think we've gone as far as we can."

Jade's breath left her. "Surely you don't mean that," she whispered.

"I'm sorry but I have to go," Lucas said, running his hand on his face.

"Lucas…"

"Jade, please," he said, his tone pained.

She bit her lip, then leaned over to kiss him on the cheek. "Okay," she said softly.

Then she got out of the car and watched him leave.

She didn't believe it was over. Lucas simply needed some time alone to process what she'd just revealed to him.

She wished she could be by his side while he worked it all out in his head. It couldn't be easy for him, and she wanted to be there to hold him and kiss him and comfort him. But she felt that Lucas wanted to make sense of things by himself. He needed his space.

Hopefully, in a couple of weeks, he'd be ready to let her back in.

She'd be anxiously waiting.

CHAPTER TWELVE

Lucas opened his suitcase and started packing.

Why the hell did he feel so damned lost?

"Because you're a fucking moron," he muttered.

He might as well be honest with himself. Jade had stuck a knife to his heart and twisted it.

This was precisely why he didn't want relationships and all that shit. Too complicated, too consuming, too… hurtful.

Sure, there were great times—the sex, the tender moments, the laughter…

He shook his head, refusing to remember them. They weren't real. How could they be when on Jade's part it was all an act?

The fact that she took their breakup so calmly, as if it were nothing—as if *they* had been *nothing* to each other—was further proof that her affections were fake.

His eyes stung and he angrily wiped away a tear.

After his conversation with Rick and Connor yesterday, he'd thought long and hard about confronting Jade about whether she was Thomas' willing puppet. He'd decided to give her the benefit of the doubt.

But in the end, her words and actions gave her away.

He should have doubted Jade's I-know-nothing act from the beginning, instead of being quick to believe everything she'd said. For all he knew, even the fact that she'd become Ruby's customer was part of the plan.

He stilled. His mother would naturally continue being friends with Jade if he didn't interfere. Should he, though?

With him going away for two weeks, and with Jade going to Greg's surprise party with his mum on the weekend, it would play on his mind that Jade's friendship with Ruby might be fake, too. It would drive him crazier. He'd need to find an answer soon.

There was only one option he could think of that was available to him right now.

He went to his spare room and opened a desk drawer. The card that Jade had handed to him a couple weeks ago was right on the top of the pile. He picked it up and turned it over. Then he dialled the private number handwritten on it.

"Hello?" came a wary reply.

"Mr. Bilton?"

"Yes. Who's this?"

"It's Lucas Renner."

*****

Lucas took a deep breath before pressing the call button on the security pad by the gate.

"Good evening, Mr. Renner," greeted a male voice. "Please drive through to the top of the driveway. Mr. Bilton will be waiting for you by the front of the house."

He thanked the man and waited until the gates were fully opened before cruising in, still marvelling at the fact that Thomas had agreed to see him at ten o'clock at night.

It surprised him that Thomas had seemed pleased and eager for this encounter. He'd expected the man to decline—or at least ask for a more reasonable meeting time.

He followed the curve of the driveway and found Thomas standing by the entrance of the impressive house. His heart pounded. For the first time, he'd be face to face with his biological father. It was surreal.

He stopped the car and got out.

"Lucas," Thomas said, surprising him once again. He'd expected 'Mr. Renner'.

"Welcome," Thomas continued. "I'm pleased to finally meet you in person."

"Thank you for seeing me at such a late hour, Mr. Bilton," he said politely.

"Please, call me Thomas, at least."

His lips twisted. "I'd rather not, sir."

Thomas gave him a sad smile, disconcerting him for a second. He gave himself a mental shake.

"Please come in."

Lucas followed Thomas into the house and looked around for security men. He found none, although he was sure that cameras were strategically placed everywhere.

He hid a smirk. If he'd come with a knife or a gun to threaten Thomas Bilton, he would have been successful. Not that he'd ever do anything like that. He was just astounded, yet again, that how he'd pictured this meeting wasn't what was happening. He'd thought someone would

127

frisk him for weapons before being allowed to see Thomas.

Thomas opened the door to a room at the back of the house.

"Welcome to my personal man-cave," Thomas said. "I believe that's what you young people call it these days."

Lucas walked in, his mouth parting in pleasant surprise. There was a large desk on one side and a massive flat screen on the wall opposite it. But his eyes were drawn to the sports memorabilia hanging on the wall. Even from where he was standing, he could see how valuable the pieces were. He was sure he'd find them to be limited edition items autographed by famous sports figures in their respective fields. He hated to say it, but this was his kind of room.

"Please feel free to check them out," Thomas said softly, noticing his interest.

"Maybe later, sir," he said. "Perhaps we should begin our conversation? It's late."

"Of course," Thomas said. "Please take a seat on the sofa. Would you like tea, coffee, juice? I won't offer you wine or beer as you'll be driving back."

Lucas had to smile at that comment. "Nothing for me, thank you."

"Please, Lucas. Have something."

"Coffee then, please. Flat white, no sugar," he answered. Perhaps the ambiance of this room was tempering his emotions.

Thomas rushed to his desk and pressed a button on an intercom next to it. "Please bring the refreshments in, Karen. Mr. Renner will have a flat white, no sugar." Then he sat on an adjacent chair and smiled at Lucas. "I've seen recent photos of you on your social media pages. You look exactly like them."

Lucas chuckled. He had to admit, if Thomas was working on getting him to let his guard down, he was doing a great job of it. He'd have to watch himself.

"You're a bit older than the last picture I've seen of you, sir," he said.

Thomas laughed. "I avoid having my photo taken these days."

"Well, Mr. Bilton. I'm glad we've started this conversation on a genial tone," he said, deciding it was time to get to the point. "I'm here to reiterate and assure you that my mother and I won't create any trouble. We haven't for thirty years, and we're not about to start now. All I'm asking is to close whatever book is still open and get on with our lives."

"Has Jade told you about our meeting yesterday?"

The knife in Lucas' heart twisted at the mention of Jade's name. "Yes. To be perfectly frank, sir. I don't buy it."

Thomas let out a big sigh.

"There's no need for all this scheming, Mr. Bilton. I'd even offer to sign a nondisclosure agreement myself. Needless to say, you also have to keep quiet about my mother's past."

They were interrupted by a knock.

"Come in," Thomas called loudly.

The door opened and in walked a woman in housekeeper uniform. She placed a tray on the table, filled with a small fresh fruit platter, pastries, a cup of coffee and a pot of tea.

"Thank you," they murmured to the housekeeper, who poured Thomas' tea before walking out quietly.

"Lucas, what exactly do you think I'm trying to protect?" Thomas asked softly. "Why do you think I'm doing what you think I'm doing?"

Lucas stared at Thomas. Did he really need to point it out?

He raked his hair. He was here to put the matter to bed. It was time to stop dancing around the main issue and lay everything on the table.

"For years you left us alone," he said, holding Thomas' gaze. "Then the news broke about five months ago that an employee of a certain escort agency has started naming her married politician clients. In an interview, the woman called on past and present escorts to name and shame the married politicians who'd paid for sex. That woman worked for the same agency that connected you to my mum."

"Your mother told you that story?" Thomas asked in surprise.

"Yes, she did. Now, you're not a politician, but you're high profile and you were engaged when you met Mum. When your henchman turned up on Mum's doorstep a few months ago, I figured it was because you've decided to remind her of your agreement, in case she was thinking of following the suggestions of the woman in the news. But I can guarantee you she has no intentions of creating a scandal involving you, Mr. Bilton."

Thomas shook his head emphatically. "Lucas, I didn't send anyone."

Lucas threw up his hands in frustration. "Mr. Bilton, I don't know what else to say to you to put your mind at ease that your secret is safe. No one will know you had a child with a woman you met through an escort agency while you were engaged to Diana. My mother doesn't want that to come out either. Although she was one of a few who had a strict no-sex policy when she worked as an escort, who'd believe her if she explained that she became pregnant because you'd started dating, and not because you were her client? She knows that there are certain sections of society that would have some judgement on that. She wants to protect me as well as her business. So she—we—are not going to blab the past to anyone. And for the record, I am not, and will not be, after your money. I'll put that in writing if it makes you feel better."

"Oh, Lucas," Thomas said, suddenly looking fragile and emotional. He stood up and went to his computer. The big screen on the wall came to life. "Please have a look."

Lucas frowned but he sat on another chair to see the screen better.

"I know Jade would have told you everything I told her yesterday. You say you don't buy it. But please pay attention to these."

Thomas clicked his mouse and a document on a prominent law firm's letterhead appeared on the screen. It was dated three months ago. Lucas read it and he covered his mouth in shock.

"As you can see," Thomas said. "I threatened to sue the clinic who did the paternity test. The result I was given was fake. It stated you're not my child. But this letter from the clinic's lawyers proved that they didn't make a mistake—that they sent the correct results to your mother and to my assistant, who I'd asked to coordinate the matter. I never knew until four months ago that you are my child, Lucas."

Lucas slumped on the seat, his eyes watering.

"And here are the emails I've been exchanging with the private detective who's working to figure out who has been harassing your mother. He tells me his work would be much easier if he could talk to you and Ruby. But I didn't want him to contact you until I'd spoken to you. I was afraid I'll alienate you further."

Thomas scrolled slowly through various emails, allowing Lucas to follow the discussion in each. Lucas saw the extent of Thomas' incredulity and fury at discovering the deception that had gone on for many years. His eyes bulged out when he saw how much money Thomas had offered the private detective to get to the bottom of the matter as fast as possible.

"I can give you all these documents, Lucas. If you feel the need, you can get experts to confirm their authenticity."

Lucas had to admit it was compelling evidence. He couldn't ignore the fact that these proved Thomas was telling the truth.

Thomas walked back to join him on the sofa. "When I received the original paternity result—the fake one—I did send someone to talk to Ruby and ask to her to stop scamming me. I did tell my assistant to threaten to expose her for fraudulent activities regarding the pregnancy if she divulged our affair to anyone. But that was the extent of my communication with her. I didn't hear back from your mother after that and I thought that was the end of it."

Lucas stared at Thomas, remembering Jade's comment regarding Thomas' demeanour when the two of them had spoken. Jade was right. Looking at the man, all he could sense were honesty, pain, regret and confusion. After he'd given Thomas his absolute guarantee of his silence, there was no reason for Thomas to keep persisting with his charade—unless it truly wasn't an act.

He took an involuntary breath, feeling a lightening in his chest.

"The one thing I've wondered, Lucas, every single day since knowing this, is why Ruby never told me. Why did she stay quiet?" Thomas asked, his eyes troubled.

"I'd wondered about the same thing," he answered. "Mum used to work two, three jobs at a time so she could buy me nice presents and clothes and send me to good schools. Child support from you would have made her life a lot easier. But she said that the threat your assistant made was not only to expose her stint at the escort agency but also to take me away from her. She was scared into believing that because she'd been an escort, you could easily get the courts to grant you full custody of me. It was even suggested to her that you might take me to another country and she'd never see me again. In exchange for her silence, she was promised that you'd leave us alone."

"Oh my God," Thomas whispered, clearly appalled. "I most certainly would have demanded to be part of your life, and at the very least pay child support. I was a cocky bastard back then, Lucas, but I would never have turned my back on my own son." Thomas paused, wiping a stray tear. "I want to make up for all the years we've lost. I want you to be part of my life, my company... everything."

"You hardly know me, sir," Lucas croaked past the lump in his throat.

"I know enough, Lucas. And nothing changes the fact that you are my own flesh and blood. My *only* child. You may not believe this, but I do love you as if I've known you all your life."

Lucas took a deep breath, trying to contain his emotions. He stared at Thomas, and a tear fell.

His father had never rejected him. His mother was not treated like a nobody. Thomas didn't know.

He dropped his head in his hands and let the cathartic tears flow.

When he lifted his head, Thomas was silently weeping. He reached for his father's hand and squeezed. Thomas pulled him for a tight hug, and with that gesture, he felt the healing begin.

"When did you find out I was your father?" Thomas asked when they'd composed themselves.

"When I was sixteen I needed to get a passport," he answered. "It was the first time I saw my birth certificate. It named Thomas Bilton as my father. Before that I'd always believed that my father's name was Thomas Renner and that he was dead. I questioned Mum. She tried to avoid telling me for the longest time. Then one day, she sat me down and told me everything. She'd worried I might hate her. To the contrary, I saw her deep love for me. I totally understood why she did what she did. Unfortunately, those untruths also made me hate you."

"I'm so sorry about all this," Thomas said. "I'd like to personally apologise to your mother, Lucas."

"I'm off to Japan early tomorrow and I'm there for two weeks. I'll talk to her about this first thing when I come back. I'll tell her you want to talk to her."

"Thank you, son," Thomas whispered.

Lucas smiled. "I want to warn you that I'm not a 'yes' person. I can be headstrong, argumentative and difficult."

Thomas chuckled. "I wouldn't expect anything less."

"Um… about Jade…" Lucas said, already guessing Thomas' answer. But he had to confirm.

"Yes?"

"You really didn't tell her anything until yesterday, right?"

"That's right. Like I said, I didn't want her to know what you didn't want her to know. So I waited until you'd spoken with her."

Lucas nodded.

"I'm very grateful to her," Thomas said. "I don't think I would have gotten anywhere with you if it weren't for her. Even for getting you to read that first letter and listen to my recording, she already deserves an extra-special bonus."

"Have you given her any yet?" he asked casually.

"She doesn't know it but I've ordered a car," Thomas said with a grin. "Not a company car, but all hers. And it's one that I heard her say in passing that she dreams of having."

Lucas breathed a sigh of relief. Jade had been honest with him.

And he'd been an absolute idiot. The biggest of the lot.

"I plan to surprise her with the car in a few days," Thomas said. "It would be great if you could be around when I give her the keys."

"You might scare her off with something so grand this early in her employment. She might feel too uncomfortable." Lucas was certain that Jade would feel awkward getting the car just after he'd broken up with her. He didn't want her to have any negative feelings towards her dream BMW.

"Really? I never thought of that. What do you suggest?"

"Still give her the car, but maybe around Christmas when bonuses are usually handed out." That would give him plenty of time to apologise and grovel. Hopefully it wouldn't take that long for Jade to forgive him.

"Good idea," Thomas said, nodding his head. "I'll ask for the order to be put on hold and released closer to Christmas."

Lucas hid his smile, knowing Rick would get annoyed by that. Oh, well.

"Was there something you kept from her?" Thomas asked.

"She doesn't know about Mum's past at the escort agency. I figured that's up to Mum to decide whether to tell her or not."

"I didn't mention that to her, either," Thomas confirmed.

"Do you mind if you don't tell her about this conversation until I come back?"

"Of course," Thomas said. "Lucas, I don't mean to pry, but are you two going out?"

He inhaled deeply. "We were. But I messed up big time."

"Oh. Jade's a nice a girl. She's a keeper, you know. I hope you work it out."

A keeper.

If Lucas chased after Jade now it would loudly signal one thing—that he was ready for a serious, committed relationship.

Yes, he was more than halfway there. In fact he was almost certain of it. But he wanted to be one hundred percent sure of what he truly wanted before doing anything. He didn't want to stuff Jade around.

Perhaps going away for two weeks was a blessing in disguise. He had that time to think.

CHAPTER THIRTEEN

Jade looked around for Ruby after taking a breather from dancing. Like Ruby, she'd been apprehensive that she'd feel out of place. Surprisingly, Greg's party had a very down-to-earth feel.

Sure, there was glamour and gourmet food and fancy decor, but everyone she'd met had been wonderful and friendly. The ambiance and happy mood of the celebrations lifted her spirits considerably.

After Lucas had broken up with her two nights ago, she'd been down in the dumps. She couldn't wait until he got back to Australia so she could have a long talk with him. He'd said he wasn't after a relationship, but she bet that was just an excuse. She was sure that what made him distance himself was her forcing him onto Thomas Bilton—a man Lucas didn't trust yet.

Just because she was Thomas Bilton's PA didn't mean they couldn't make it work as a couple. Besides, she was sure that once Lucas agreed to giving Thomas a chance to explain, he'd come around to opening his heart to the man who was trying everything to connect with him. And she wouldn't give up on helping Thomas for Lucas and Ruby's sake.

She spotted Ruby, who looked like she was having the time of her life, laughing out loud while chatting with Greg's grandmother. She smiled, happy to see Ruby comfortable with 'the rich and famous'.

If it weren't for Jade's heavy heart, she'd be having the time of her life, too. It was difficult hiding her pain from everybody, but so far, she'd been succeeding.

She walked to join Rick, not wanting to interrupt Ruby.

Even though she was supposed to be Rick's plus one, she'd hardly spoken to him at all. He seemed a little distant tonight compared to his friendliness at the pub. She could understand, though. Rick probably wanted to party with his family and friends rather than entertain someone he hardly knew.

"Hi, Rick," she said.

"Hey, Jade. Enjoying the night?" Rick asked.

"Yes, it's great. Thanks again for taking me," she said teasingly.

Rick smiled, then introduced her to his friends Connor and Amanda. "Connor used to work with Lucas for the same Formula One team," Rick said. "He's the one who introduced Lucas to me and my famous cousins."

"Oh, right," she said, happy to meet another one of Lucas' friends. "Lucas has told me about your plans to be business partners, Connor," she said conversationally.

"Has he? Yeah. I'm just waiting for the man to make the decision. We've agreed it can only work if we're both working full-time on the business. We don't want to mess up our friendship."

"At least he's not considering setting up a rival car servicing shop," Rick said with a snicker.

The guys laughed.

"Connor and Lucas are great buddies who enjoy competing with each other," Amanda said with an eyeroll.

"Oh, really?" Jade said with a smile.

"Yeah, Lucas even tried to steal Amanda from me," Connor said. "As you can see, I won, 'cause she's now my wife."

Jade chuckled, certain that Connor was joking.

"Did I hear Lucas' name mentioned?" a stunning woman said, joining their little group. "Where is Mr. Fuck King anyway? How come he's not here tonight?"

Jade raised her eyebrows. What did this woman call Lucas?

"He's in Japan for work," Connor answered.

"Ah. Shame. He's missing out on a great party. No doubt he's having fun in Japan with his girls there, though."

Then Miss Stunning turned to Jade. "Hi, I'm Marilyn."

"I'm Jade," she said with a wan smile.

"How do you know the birthday boy, Jade? Or are you one of Gemma's friends?"

"No. I'm… Rick brought me here."

"Oh!" Marilyn said, looking at Rick with disbelieving eyes.

"Don't look so shocked, Marilyn. Jade's just a friend," Rick said with a laugh.

Marilyn chuckled. "That's a relief. Since Greg proposed to Gemma tonight, some of us girls thought it would be fun to have a bet."

"What are you betting on?" Rick asked.

"Which among you bachelors would be the next one to be captured by *looove*," Marilyn said theatrically. "I have my money on Simon. So don't you dare go finding yourself a girlfriend."

"You're money's safe, darlin'," Rick said with a laugh.

"Who are the others betting on?" Amanda asked.

"I can't remember exactly, but there's at least one bet for Simon, Derek, Keith and Tristan. No one bet on Rick and Lucas. None of us wants to lose."

"Smart girls," Connor quipped. "You could also have a long-term bet on who will be the last one standing."

"That was the original bet," Marilyn said with a laugh. "Everyone said it would be Lucas. No one dared pick anyone other than the reigning Mr. Fuck King. We all know he's not like you, Connor. So we changed it around. It should be more fun picking who'd be hit next by Cupid's arrow anyway."

Jade felt her whole body heat up. Was Marilyn really talking about *her* Lucas? And what on earth did being Mr. Fuck King mean?

She gave a token wave to Marilyn when Miss Stunning left their little circle.

"You want a drink, Jade?" Rick asked.

She started to shake her head, already nearing her limit, then changed her mind. "Yes, please. A glass of white." She had a feeling she'd need it.

When Rick went to get the drinks, she casually asked Connor and Amanda, "Was Marilyn talking about Lucas *Renner* as Mr. Fuck King?"

"Yes," Connor said.

"How did he end up being called that?"

Amanda snickered, looking pointedly at Connor.

Connor pulled his wife to him and kissed her on the temple.

"Connor used to hold the title," Amanda said with a giggle. "His buddies on the tour bestowed it on him."

"Then I met Amanda and it ended up with Lucas," Connor said.

"What does it mean?" Jade asked.

"Uh, it means he's very popular with the ladies wherever in the world he is," Connor said.

It seemed to Jade that she just got a sanitised version of the truth. "You mean he's popular with the ladies *in bed*?" she asked for clarification.

"Yes," Connor said.

"Mind you," Amanda said. "Lucas tried hard to wrestle it away from Connor."

"How?" she asked, dreading the answer.

"Well, a lot depended on how... uh... happy he made the ladies," Connor said, clearly uncomfortable.

"I see," Jade said, although she couldn't believe it.

*

Jade hid a sigh when Ruby went to the dance floor. That meant they weren't leaving yet.

She truly appreciated that everyone was being so friendly and welcoming but, quite frankly, she was ready to go home. She just didn't feel like being around anyone anymore after what she'd learned about Lucas.

She'd thought he just got mad at her because of Thomas, but he must have meant every single word he'd said in the car when he dumped her.

'I'm not after a relationship, Jade. I never have been. I think we've gone as far as we can.'

Ouch. Those lines hurt more now than they originally did.

"Jade!"

Marilyn was waving to her to come over.

She smiled, hoping it didn't look fake. Hopefully there would be no conversation about Lucas amongst the group she was about to join.

"This is Jade, Rick's friend," Marilyn said to the other women.

Jade smiled pleasantly as Marilyn made introductions. She'd given up trying to remember the names of each person she'd met. It was impossible.

"Did you arrive with Rick?" a blonde asked. "I though he was alone when he got here."

"I actually got a lift from Ruby—that lady over there," she answered, pointing towards Ruby's direction.

"Isn't that Lucas' mother?" asked a brunette who was wearing the most revealing outfit of the night.

"Yes."

"How come you came with her when you're Rick's plus one?" the brunette persisted.

"Ruby and I are friends. It was just more convenient."

"Oh, really? Maybe you can introduce me to her."

Marilyn laughed. "Why, Vicky? Are you hoping to enlist Ruby's help to get Lucas to turn over a new leaf?"

Vicky flicked her hair, smiling in a way that said she knew something.

Jade decided she didn't like this Vicky person.

"Do you know that Lucas is in Japan?" Marilyn said.

"Yeah, so?" Vicky asked.

"So are you hoping that he won't be hopping into anyone's bed there?"

Vicky rolled her eyes. "Come on. I'm not deluded. That would be hoping for the impossible. But I do think that for someone like Lucas, a balancing act is what's necessary."

"Balancing act?" said another girl.

Jade was glad the question was asked. She wanted to know what Vicky meant, too.

"You have to give certain types of men some freedom," Vicky said. "The important thing is, when he's ready to commit to someone, you're at the top of his list."

"So will you be putting money on Lucas to be the next one to be captured by love, Vicky?" the blonde asked.

Vicky snorted. "Like I said, I'm not deluded. But I'm biding my time."

"Hope you have extra years in your life to spare," Marilyn said with sarcasm.

Vicky laughed.

Jade wanted to cry.

CHAPTER FOURTEEN

"Are you all right, Mum?" Lucas asked, peering at his mother with concern.

Ruby continued to stare at him mutely, ashen, with eyes like saucers.

He took Ruby's hand and rubbed it. "From everything I've seen, Mum, he's telling the truth," he said softly.

With a sudden, shaky breath, as if startled from a dream, Ruby squeezed his hand. "He accepts you as his son?" she whispered.

He nodded.

"In exchange for what?"

"Nothing, Mum. Nothing."

"Did he make you sign anything? As guarantee you won't contest whatever's in his will when he leaves his fortune to other people?"

He smiled. His mother was thinking what he used to believe about Thomas. "He actually wants me to have a look around Bilton Machineries to see if it would interest me to be a part of it."

"Oh. And do you think you'll be interested?"

"I've thought about it a lot in the last couple of weeks," he said, his enthusiasm bubbling. "It does interest me that the business is about machineries. Very different from cars, of course, but they're very much into technical development and improvement. They're expanding to other areas outside of construction, too. They're opening up a department to focus on new inventions to make sure the company takes advantage of advancements in technology. There are a lot of exciting things happening there at the moment."

"What about Formula One?"

"Well, my boss told me he couldn't agree to the limited number of days I'm asking for. My choice is to keep my current schedule or quit the team. I've taken annual leave so I can think about this before making my final decision. But right now, I'm leaning towards the new challenge Bilton Machineries could give."

"So Thomas is really happy to give you a job in his company?"

"Well, I still feel uncomfortable about it, but he insists I'm his heir."

Ruby's jaw slackened, then tears rushed down her cheeks. "Oh, darling. If he really means it, then I'm so glad for you. You deserve it, Lucas."

He hugged his mother.

His future with Bilton Machineries was far from settled. Anything could happen while he and his father worked on their relationship. For all he knew, things might not work as Thomas had planned.

But he found great enthusiasm for the company that he hadn't thought he'd ever have. He suspected it had always been in him though, and that it had just been buried underneath pain and anger.

Ever since he found out who his father was, he'd secretly followed news about Thomas Bilton. While personal details got his blood boiling, developments in Bilton Machineries had always held his attention. He guessed it was a genes thing. He and Thomas shared the love for machineries of different kinds and how they could be used to impact people's lives.

He never thought he'd feel this way about Thomas, but after clarifying their horrendous misunderstandings, he genuinely wanted to get to know him better. Perhaps there really was an indestructible bond between parents and children that couldn't be broken, no matter what the circumstances.

But first and foremost, he wanted his mother to be absolutely fine with what was happening. "Are you really okay with all this, Mum? Are you okay with me spending time with Thomas?"

"He's your father, Lucas. If his intentions come from the heart, then I'm one hundred percent okay. But if this is a trick and he messes with you, he better hide. All my claws will come out."

Lucas laughed, relieved. "He wants to talk to you," he murmured. "Are you comfortable with that?"

Ruby hesitated, but eventually she nodded.

"Great. I'm due to visit Thomas'—Dad's—office today. I'll arrange it and let you know."

"Okay," Ruby said, concern appearing on her face again. "Is there any news on that man who came to harass me? Or who he really is?"

"Private investigators are working on it. I'll be speaking with them tomorrow to give them description and some information. It'll probably help if they talk to you too. Would you be okay with that?"

"Yes," Ruby said with determination, her eyes steeling. "Whoever sent that man is responsible for years of heartache and pain. I want to know who they are and why they did what they did."

He nodded. He wanted that, too. "We'll get to the bottom of this soon," he said, rubbing Ruby's arms.

Ruby nodded, giving him another hug.

He returned the embrace, praying that this matter could be put to bed. If anyone deserved happiness, it was Ruby Renner.

"So how was Greg's party?" he asked, diverting into something lighter.

"Oh, it was wonderful!" Ruby said, her face splitting from remembered fun. "Did you know that he proposed to his girlfriend on the night? It was very sweet."

"Yeah. I got several messages from the guys," he said with a laugh. "I rang Greg and Gemma when I found out."

"Jade and I had a fantastic time, although the poor girl had a bad headache by the end of the night. I think she had too much to drink."

"Have you seen Jade since?" he asked, his heartbeat accelerating from saying her name.

"No. She's due to get her flowers in a couple of days, though, so I'll see her then."

"Okay."

He kissed his mother goodbye and started walking to the Bilton Machineries building. He didn't know what made him more nervous: walking around his father's company for the first time or convincing Jade to talk to him.

*****

Lucas pinned the visitor's tag the receptionist gave him on the breast pocket of his shirt, then he rode the elevator to the top floor. He took deep breaths as the lift zoomed up to his destination.

How would Jade react to his presence? Frankly, he wouldn't be surprised if she refused to see him, or even if she slapped him. After the way he'd treated her, especially his reasons for breaking up with her, he deserved no less.

But Jade was a professional, and he was counting on her sense of duty to see him so they could have a conversation. Hopefully, it would be enough to convince her to agree to meet with him tonight for a real heart to heart.

'I think we've gone as far as we can.'

He winced as he remembered yet again that hurtful line he'd told her. What the hell had possessed him to say it? Sure, he'd been mad at her—which was totally his fault, too, because he'd assumed the wrong thing. But why say what he didn't mean?

He exhaled harshly. At the time, he'd wanted to mean it. But these last two weeks had proven something to him that he could no longer deny.

He'd fallen for Jade.

At first he believed it was just his dick leading him. But his damn cock hadn't gotten hard for any other woman since he met Jade. He'd never experienced this condition before. Those sultry women who'd tried to

149

seduce him when he was overseas couldn't even get his attention.

He missed Jade desperately. It gutted him that they'd broken up, even if it was his own stupid doing. And now he was damn scared that he'd lost all his chances.

He psyched himself as the lift doors opened, and stepped out into another reception area.

"Hello, Mr. Renner," said the smiling woman behind the desk. "Mr. Bilton is on the phone at the moment. I'll let him know you've arrived when he finishes the call."

"Thank you," he responded. "I'm a little early anyway."

"Please take a seat, sir. Can I get you tea or coffee? Or something cold, perhaps?"

"Actually, do you mind calling Jade Tully for me? There are a few things I need to see her about, too."

"Of course." The lady pressed a button. "Jade? Mr. Renner has arrived for his appointment with Mr. Bilton at eleven, but he's asked to see you now."

Lucas held his breath, wondering what Jade was thinking.

"Jade? Are you there?... Yes. Mr. Lucas Renner... Yes... Really? It's right here on my calendar. It's strange it's not showing on yours... Thanks."

"She'll be right with you in a second, Mr. Renner," the receptionist said.

"Thank you," he said, glad his dad had managed to hide this appointment from Jade. He'd requested it so Jade couldn't call in sick or something, just to avoid him.

He felt her before he saw her. He turned to his left and saw Jade standing there. She looked as shocked as his mother had been earlier.

"Hi," he said, the word coming out like a sigh as his heart pounded hard.

"Mr. Renner," Jade said, clearly trying to sound unflustered. "I didn't know Mr. Bilton was expecting you."

"He is. At eleven. But since he's still on a phone call, I thought we could start discussing a few things," he said, going for a professional tone even though all he wanted to do was take her in his arms and kiss her.

"I see… Um…"

"Meeting room one is free," the helpful receptionist said. "I'll inform Mr. Bilton— Oh wait. It looks like he's off the phone. Shall I let him know—"

"Yes, please, Ann," Jade said hastily, to Lucas' consternation.

He stared at Jade while the receptionist spoke to his father. But Jade kept her gaze on Ann, refusing to look at him.

God, he missed her.

"Jade," Ann said. "Mr. Bilton wants you to take Mr. Renner to his office. I'm to fix the refreshments so you can sit in on their meeting."

"Okay," Jade said weakly. "Please follow me, Mr. Renner."

Lucas obeyed, hoping he didn't just make her madder for springing this on her.

CHAPTER FIFTEEN

Jade walked as calmly as she could as she led Lucas to Thomas' office. She had no idea what to expect, or what she'd do if Lucas started going off at Thomas. Surely he had no plans to do that?

She glanced at him from the corner of her eye, only to avert her gaze quickly. He was looking right at her.

"Jade," he whispered.

Her breathing almost stopped at the caressing tone of his voice.

Ugh. Don't be a fool, Jade Tully.

She bet Mr. Fuck King didn't even think about her while he was away. Well, she supposed she could thank him for breaking up with her first. At least he had the decency to do that.

Thomas' office door opened and she tried to swallow her nerves. She hoped this would be an amicable—

"Lucas!" Thomas exclaimed in pleasure.

"Hello, sir," Lucas said.

To Jade's utter shock the two men embraced.

"When we get a few things sorted out, you can call me Dad in public," Thomas said in a low but authoritative voice.

"Ordering me around already, I see," Lucas said dryly, humour lacing his tone.

Thomas chuckled while Jade stood frozen.

What the hell is going on?

"Jade, sit in with us, please," Thomas said warmly, gesturing for her to walk in first.

"Do you mind if I have a minute alone with Jade before we start the meeting?" Lucas asked Thomas.

"Oh, of course. How long do you need?"

"I know you're both busy so a couple of minutes would be fine, thank you."

"Well, I might go to the bathroom then," Thomas said, walking away.

"Jade..." Lucas said when Thomas had disappeared.

"You've spoken with him," she said softly, truly pleased at this surprising development.

"Yes. And you were right. I believe him now, too."

She smiled. "I'm really glad, Lucas."

"Jade, this is not the time for the two of us to talk. But can I see you tonight, please? There's so much I need to say to you."

"Sorry. I'm not free tonight."

Lucas took a deep breath. "Okay. Tomorrow?"

She shook her head. For the last two weeks since Greg's birthday, she'd been working on moving on from him. What she'd heard from his friends at the party, coupled with what he'd said when he'd unceremoniously dumped her, gave her a sense of closure. It didn't make it any easier, nor did it lessen the pain, but it erased all perceptions of hope that she could have hung on to. It was evident that a future with him was highly unlikely.

She was doing well despite her still-aching heart, so she wouldn't do anything that might undo the fruits of her emotional hard work. She'd end up being too pathetic otherwise.

"So when can we meet, Jade?" Lucas said.

His beseeching tone made her look up into his eyes. There was plea in them and she felt herself start to melt—

Don't you fucking dare, Jade Tully!

"Sorry, Lucas," she said in a clear voice. "My calendar's a bit full for social stuff."

"Jade, please. There's a lot I need to explain."

"No need, Lucas," she said with a wide smile. "And I'm so thrilled that you and Mr. Bilton have worked out your differences."

Lucas stared at her in consternation.

"Does Ruby know?" she asked gently.

"Yes. I told her this morning. I haven't told her about your involvement yet, though. I thought we should do it together."

She nodded. That, she'd be happy to do.

"So why do I need to sit in on this meeting?" she asked.

"Dad's very appreciative of your help. Since you didn't know until a few minutes ago that the two of us have spoken, we thought you should join us. We'll be discussing the man who's been harassing Mum, and Dad planned to show me around here today. We're not telling anyone yet that I'm his son, though. That won't be until we finalise everything about this matter and catch the culprit."

"I hope you catch whoever's responsible soon," she said with feeling. "It's reprehensible what they've done."

"Do you need more time?" Thomas interrupted, walking back into the room.

"We're fine, Mr. Bilton," she answered, ignoring Lucas' heavy sigh.

*****

Jade sat on the couch, staring at the phone in her hand.

"Hey, that thing's gonna melt if you don't quit eyeballing it," Lexie said.

"Huh?" Jade asked, looking up at her friend.

"Uh-oh," Erin said, putting down her cup of ice cream. "Who texted you?"

"It's nothing," Jade said with a little shake of the head.

"It must be something then," Cassie said knowingly. "Come on, share."

Jade sighed. "Lucas is back."

"And?" the three said in unison.

She shrugged. "He wants to see me."

"Well, you know what to do," Cassie said. "Text him back and tell him you're busy."

"I've already told him that today."

"You've already spoken to him today?" Erin asked.

Jade groaned silently. She really needed to talk to Lucas and Thomas about her NDA. Since things with father and son were starting to look promising, perhaps they wouldn't mind if she told her friends?

Not that she didn't trust these three women to keep a secret. Apart from her family, there were no other people she trusted more. But it was out of respect for Lucas, Ruby and Thomas that she hadn't breathed a word of their issues to anyone.

So for now, she'd limited her stories around the fact that Lucas was Ruby's son, and that they had a brief relationship which had ended because Lucas had said 'they'd gone as far as they can'.

She sniffed without meaning to. Damn it. That sentence still packed a punch.

"What did you talk about today, Jade?" Lexie pressed softly.

"He said there's a lot he wants to explain."

"Like why he's called Mr. Fuck King?" Cassie said sarcastically. "I still think he's a cad for making you believe he's so into you when all he was after was sex."

"And only telling you on the day he dumped you that he wasn't looking for a relationship," Erin reminded her. "To think that his mum sounds like a nice woman."

To Jade's annoyance, her eyes watered.

"Hey," Erin said softly. "Remember you want us to keep telling you why it's a bad idea to entertain thoughts of getting back together with him?"

Jade nodded. Her friends meant well. "Don't you think I should at least see why he's being so persistent?" she couldn't help asking. "What if he's got something really important to say?"

"Like what?"

Like he missed her, like he was sorry, like…

Ah, damn. She was in danger of regressing just from seeing him this morning.

"You're right," she said with renewed determination. "He was very clear why he broke up with me. And those friends of his who call him Mr. Fuck King must know him much better than I do. If even they don't believe that Lucas is the type to commit to one woman, what are the chances that *I* could make him? Minuscule—if that," she said, answering her own question.

"I think you should get straight back on the dating circuit," Cassie said. "Don't let this experience destroy the self-confidence you've just gained."

"You know what?" Erin said. "Not that I want you to relive painful memories, but I suppose you could at least thank Lucas for helping you break through your fear that you're someone a man leaves after just one night. You were hardly home when you were seeing him."

Jade blushed, remembering their hot nights, often with multiple orgasms. Yes, she could thank Lucas for lifting her self-confidence in the sexual arena.

But she'd honestly thought that the reason why sex with him was out of this world was because they also shared a strong emotional connection. Well, perhaps that had been the case with her. For his part, she guessed he was just great in bed—like many of his sexual partners could probably attest.

"Why don't you go out with Gordon?" Lexie asked. "He's got the hots for you and doesn't care who knows."

"Is this the new assistant manager in your marketing team?" Erin asked.

"Yep. He's really keen on Jade. He only just joined the company and he's already clearly besotted with her."

Jade snorted. "I wouldn't say asking me to go out for drinks is being *clearly besotted.*"

"He wanders around your floor during working hours for no reason other than to see you," Lexie said with a laugh. "He doesn't even care what Mr. Bilton would think. For a man whose job isn't secure yet, he sure has guts. I call that clearly besotted."

"How did you know he goes up to our floor?" Jade asked.

"Because he told me. He knows I'm one of your best friends so he's being extra friendly with me."

"Ooh, I say give the man a chance, Jade," Erin said.

"And give yourself a chance," Cassie added. "Lucas was never the right man. Train your sights elsewhere."

"It's too soon. I'm not ready. And I don't want to be getting Gordon's hopes up."

"Why don't you start as friends?" Lexie said. "Make it clear to Gordon that you're not ready for a relationship, but that you're happy to enjoy lunches or coffees as friends. If you give yourself that opportunity, you just might find that he's a decent guy and you wouldn't mind dating him officially."

"Not to mention show Lucas you're not sitting around moping because of him," Cassie said. "His ego doesn't deserve to be stroked like that."

"I guess you girls have a point," Jade mused. She didn't have anything to lose and much to gain.

158

*****

"Hi."

Jade's heart raced before she even looked up. "Hi," she said to Lucas. "Ann didn't buzz to say that you've arrived."

"She said Mr. Bilton has instructed her to ask me to just walk in," Lucas said.

Her lips twitched. Ann was wandering about, and she knew Lucas was careful to call his father 'Mr. Bilton'.

It sounded strange now to hear him say that. The speed with which the relationship between the two had progressed was heartwarming.

She picked up the phone to let Thomas know Lucas had arrived. But at that moment, the system signalled that Thomas got on the line.

"It looks like he just called someone," she said. "Do you mind waiting for a minute? He's expecting you so I'm sure he won't be long at all."

"Can I sit here, then?" Lucas asked, indicating to her visitor's chair.

"Of course," she said. What else could she say?

"Are you joining us for lunch?" Lucas asked.

"No."

"Why not? Mr. Bilton invited you, right?"

"He's confirmed though that it's not necessary for me to be there."

Lucas exhaled loudly. "Jade—"

"I'd just rather get involved with business matters this time around, Lucas," she said softly.

There was that pleading look in his eyes again.

159

Ugh. What did it mean?

She looked down at her desk, pretending to fiddle with some papers. It was critical for her to get used to being around him without being affected. Thomas had confided that Lucas was seriously considering a role at Bilton Machineries, so it seemed she'd be seeing a lot of him at work from now on.

"He's off the phone now," she said, seeing the indicator light next to her boss's name disappear. "Just walk straight in."

"Why don't you want to talk to me?" Lucas asked softly, his gaze troubled.

"Because there's no need, Lucas," she said with a convincing smile.

Lucas frowned, staring at her for a breathless moment. Then he got up and walked to his father's office.

Jade let out the breath she didn't realise she was holding. Hopefully, Lucas would stop feeling guilty now. That was the only reason she could think of why he still persisted in wanting to see her. When he broke up with her, he obviously never anticipated that they'd bump into each other again, much less that he'd see her this frequently.

It would probably give Lucas relief if she did agree to see him. Unfortunately, she still wasn't strong enough to handle a personal conversation with him, especially when she was sure that all he wanted was to clear the air by explaining why he'd misled her. She didn't want an apology or excuse. She just wanted him to keep his distance so she could heal.

"Hey, Jade, are you ready for lunch?"

She looked up and smiled at Gordon. He was right on time. "Yes," she said, retrieving her purse from a drawer. When she stood up, Lucas and Thomas were walking out of Thomas' office and looking at them curiously.

"Hello, Mr. Bilton," Gordon said.

"Hello, Gordon," Thomas replied. "I've noticed you come up here a few times. Is everything okay in your department?"

"Yes, sir. I'm just up here to pick up Jade. I'm taking her to lunch."

"Oh. I see," Thomas said. "Well, enjoy."

"Thank you, sir," Jade and Gordon responded.

"Who's that with Mr. Bilton?" Gordon whispered when the two were out of earshot.

"Lucas Renner. They're working on some special project together."

"Oh, right. Are you ready to go?"

"Yeah."

She pretended to tidy up her desk, taking as much time as she could, before walking to the lifts with Gordon. To her consternation, Lucas and Thomas were still waiting. There was no choice but to join them.

CHAPTER SIXTEEN

Lucas clenched and unclenched his fists repeatedly as he suffered the elevator ride to the ground floor in silence. He just got why Jade didn't want to meet with him. She was going out with someone else.

Okay. That was fine. No problem. No problem at all.

Except that he wanted take this idiot Gordon by the cuff and tell him to stay away from Jade.

He took a long, deep, silent sigh. Were they sleeping together already?

The thought made him want to punch something. Anything. Preferably the man who was exchanging a quiet conversation with the woman he couldn't get out of his mind.

The lift stopped and the doors started to open.

"Enjoy your lunch, gentlemen," Gordon said before putting his hand on the small of Jade's back to escort her out.

Thomas responded in kind, but all Lucas could do was glare at the couple walking ahead of them. Jade didn't even look back.

Thomas patted his shoulder. "I'm sorry."

He frowned at his father. "Did you know about them?"

"No. This is the first time I've heard of it. Gordon's the new assistant manager in marketing. I've noticed him come up to our floor a few times. I didn't know it was because of Jade."

"Don't you have a policy against shenanigans being carried out at work?" he asked, his tone demanding.

"They were hardly shenanigans, Lucas," Thomas said dryly. "And Jade's work is not suffering. She's doing a fantastic job."

"There should be something that stops employees consorting with each other," he muttered. Oh, he knew he was being petulant. He just couldn't help himself.

Thomas chuckled. "If there were, you wouldn't be able to keep chasing after Jade when you start working at the company."

Lucas blinked. Chase after Jade. Yes, that was exactly what he wanted to do.

"What's the most effective way of chasing after a woman?" he asked. He'd never had the inclination to do it before.

"You're asking the wrong person, son. The last woman I chased was my wife Diana. That was too long ago now. The only advice I can give you is persist."

Lucas nodded. He could do that. He'd wear Jade down until she agreed to see him again. He'd show her how special she was to him. How could he give up, when she was the only woman who'd managed to capture his heart?

*****

Lucas drummed his fingers on the counter, wondering what time Jade would turn up to get her flowers. Now would be the perfect time, since his mother was busy with a bridezilla, and he'd asked Fely—Ruby's assistant—to go on an unscheduled lunch break.

His texts and phone calls to Jade had been ineffective, so he'd come up with an idea that would ensure she'd at least listen to him even for just a few minutes. And it was the perfect plan.

He'd kidnap her bunch of flowers.

He'd already asked his mother to do a bigger than usual bunch for Jade today, which Ruby didn't have a problem with after learning of Jade's part in Thomas and Lucas' reconciliation process. Then he'd carry the flowers for Jade while they walked back to her building. Except that he'd take a detour to the five-star hotel along the way and have a quiet coffee or two. Surely Jade would have to give him the time of day then? He already had his father's permission to keep Jade from work for longer than her usual lunch hour. As long as she was back before two thirty, when Thomas needed her, it was fine.

His heart lurched when Jade walked in. With Gordon.

Fuck.

He felt something shatter. Oh—that was his heart hitting the ground.

"Lucas!" Jade said. "I didn't know you'd be here today."

"Hi," he said, forcing a smile on his face.

"Hello, Lucas," Gordon said. "I didn't know you work here."

"It's my mother's shop," he said, annoyed at the man for talking to him with familiarity.

"So this is where you get your flowers from," Gordon said to Jade, surveying the place and nodding with approval. "I guess I can't surprise you with roses if I buy them from here, hey?"

Lucas had never wanted to deck a man so badly before.

"How long do you think Ruby's gonna be, Lucas?" Jade asked softly.

"I don't know. They should have been finished fifteen minutes ago."

Jade checked her watch. "Maybe I'll come back when I finish work."

"Hey, it says here they do express delivery," Gordon said, pointing to a nicely painted sign by the counter. "Why don't you get it delivered to the office, Jade?"

"I've always just taken it with me."

"I can bring it over," Lucas said. At least he'd have another chance to see her then.

Gordon frowned. "Oh. Are you the delivery guy as well?"

"No," he said with feigned politeness. "But this one will be a special delivery for Jade."

"No, I think I'd prefer to come back and pick it up later," Jade answered.

"I'll come back with you," Gordon said.

"Sure," Jade said with a smile.

Ouch. Jade had just stomped on the pieces of Lucas' heart that were still scattered on the floor.

They heard Ruby say goodbye to her client, looking exhausted.

"Will she be ordering?" Lucas asked when the customer finally left.

"She's still undecided," Ruby said with a frustrated sigh before turning to Gordon and Jade. "Hello, I'm Ruby. I'm so sorry to keep you guys waiting."

"No problem," Gordon said. "Jade's told me so much about you that I just have to see your shop for myself."

"Oh. I see," Ruby said.

Lucas felt a pinch in his chest. Gordon had heard a lot about his mother and this shop, but Gordon hadn't known he was Ruby's son. Obviously, Jade didn't even mention him to the man.

He couldn't breathe, so he excused himself, pretending he had somewhere else to go.

*

Lucas came back to the shop, relieved that Gordon was gone but sorry that Jade was, too. He found his mother sitting at the corner table, staring out the window, while Fely attended to customers.

"What's wrong, Mum?" he asked, sitting down next to her and glancing outside to where Ruby was looking. "Do you see anyone suspicious?"

"No," Ruby said, smiling at him. "Just taking a bit of a break. Bridezilla drained me of my energy."

"I say don't accept the job even if she offers it to you."

"I know," Ruby said with a sigh. "The money would be good since it sounds like it's gonna be a big wedding. But the three times she's been here, it was to interrogate me about whether I'm up to meeting her additional requirements. Yes, I think I'll pass if she decides to give me the job."

"Good idea."

"Lucas, moving on to a different topic—that man with Jade, who is he?"

"He works at Bilton Machineries, in the marketing department."

"I mean, are they going out?" Ruby asked softly, reaching to touch his arm.

"That's what it looks like," he said flatly.

Ruby smiled. "Did you wake up one day then, bang, you're in love with her?"

He took a sharp intake of breath. "I don't want to use the term love, Mum," he said a little harshly.

"Not using the term doesn't change the fact, darling."

"Using the term doesn't change facts either, Mum. Jade doesn't want to see me again. That's a fact. She's seeing someone else. That's a fact, too. What's the point of labelling it love when it's not likely to go anywhere?"

"What do you plan to do?"

He sagged on his seat, his eyes watering. "Frankly, all I want to do is keep trying until she takes me back. But what if she never will?"

*****

Lucas flashed his invitation to Ann, the receptionist at Bilton Machineries, who was manning the entrance with two other colleagues.

"Hello, Mr. Renner. Welcome to our Staff and Partners Halloween Dinner."

"Thank you, Ann."

"Please dip your hand into that men's cauldron and pick out the mask you'd like to wear for a particular game tonight."

Lucas walked towards the large vessel indicated by Ann and peered at its contents. He chuckled. Whoever organised this party had a great sense of humour.

Even though it was Halloween, the theme for the night was 'elegance' and the dress code was black tie. But the masks to choose from were cardboard cutouts of horror and cartoon characters... and Thomas Bilton.

He pulled one of his father's images.

"You're game," said Ann. "You're the first one to choose that mask."

"Really? I bet it's because everyone wants to suck up to the boss, and wearing his face won't help their cause," he said with a cheeky grin.

Ann giggled. "You could be right, Mr. Renner."

"Whose idea was this?"

"Paul Chow's. A business development manager who's moving to China to work in our new branch there. Some of the guys dared him to do something outrageous for tonight. This is what he came up with. But he'll get away with this. He brings in a lot of work to Bilton Machineries."

"Well, I do hope I'll be the only one to wear this mask tonight."

"I'd say your chances are good. Anyway, people usually place the mask on the seat of their choice so others will know it's been reserved. The tables near the stage are the most popular."

He thanked Ann and walked into the ballroom, decked elegantly in black and red motif.

"Lucas!"

Lucas grinned as he walked towards Rick, who'd been invited to this event a few times now due to his company being Thomas' car dealer of choice.

"Hey, bro," Rick said as they man-hugged. "Good to see you. I still can't believe you're here attending one of Bilton's parties. I'm still recovering from shock after what you told me yesterday."

Lucas chuckled.

"I'm really glad for you, Lucas. But I hope you find out who's behind this whole insane deception. Any news from the investigators?"

"Nothing concrete, although they assure us they're getting somewhere."

"Right," Rick said, noticing the item in Lucas's hand. "Trust you to pick that mask," Rick said with a laugh.

"What did you pick?"

"Jack O'Lantern. It's Halloween, after all. Are you sitting with Thomas tonight?"

Lucas shook is head. "People will just wonder who I am and why I'm sitting with the Biltons."

"What's your official story, if anyone asks?"

"That I'm advising Thomas on some special, top-secret project."

Rick chuckled. "I can see that working. I'm sitting over at that table. I saw a couple of attractive girls reserve their seats there. Wanna join me?"

"Actually," Lucas said, looking around, "I'd like to sit at Jade's table but not let her know until it's too late for her to switch seats. Can you help me?"

"Sure," Rick said. "It's the least I can do for planting thoughts in your head that she hadn't been honest with you."

He patted Rick's shoulder to let him know there were no hard feelings. "Did my dad cancel the car order?" he asked.

"No. He just asked for it to be delivered in December instead of now."

Lucas nodded.

"I saw Jade arrive just a few minutes ago with another girl. They placed their masks over at that table. Give me your mask and I'll save us seats next to them."

"Great. In the meantime, I'll make myself scarce so she won't see me."

*

Lucas lurked in the background as he observed the party goings-on. Almost everyone was milling around the room, feasting on canapés and sipping wine.

He hadn't seen his father arrive yet. Apparently, he and Diana usually turned up right before dinner was about to be served.

He had to say he was impressed with how Thomas ran his company. From what he could tell in the several times he'd visited the office, Thomas was a well-respected, somewhat feared boss. It was clear from how people interacted with each other that they generally liked working for Bilton Machineries.

Even tonight, he could see that the employees enjoyed socialising not only with their workmates but also the company's business partners.

His gaze didn't stray far away from Jade, though. She looked stunning in her crimson evening dress. Another glamorous woman was constantly by her side. It was most probably Lexie.

An announcement broke through the excited chatter in the room. It was time for everyone to take their seats. His father must have arrived.

He waited until Jade had gone to their table and sat.

"Time to surprise her, bro," said Rick, who appeared behind him.

Lucas lagged behind Rick, letting Jade see his friend first.

"Rick!" Jade said. "What are you doing here?"

"Hi, Jade," Rick said, taking the seat next to the woman who was probably Lexie. "I do business with Mr. Bilton. I've attended twice before."

"Oh, right. I haven't heard you mention it."

"No," Rick confirmed.

"Lexie, this is Rick. He's… uh… Greg Carmichael's cousin. Remember I went to Greg's birthday party?"

Lucas decided it was time to show himself as Rick and Lexie exchanged pleasantries.

"Hi," he said, settling himself on his seat.

Jade stared at him, aghast.

"You look great, Jade," he said softly.

"Hello, everyone," came a male voice from his other side.

It was Gordon.

"Good to see you here, Lucas," Gordon said, although Lucas didn't miss the ice in his tone.

"Hi, Gordon," Lexie said. "We were wondering when you'd get here."

"Yeah, I got held up. Anyway, there are a couple of spare seats over at my table. I thought you girls might want to join me," Gordon said, looking at Jade questioningly.

Lucas saw the play of indecision on Jade's face as she glanced at Lexie, then at Rick.

"Your choice, Jade," he said softly, his heart constricting from what it was going to be.

CHAPTER SEVENTEEN

Jade forced herself to calm down and think clearly.

She knew Lucas' name was on the guest list because she'd specifically checked if it was there. But since she didn't spot him at all during pre-dinner drinks, she'd thought he wasn't coming.

She glanced at Gordon, who was smiling at her encouragingly. If she went with him, Gordon might think she was warming to the idea of them moving past the friendship stage. She didn't want to give him that impression.

But to sit next to Lucas all through dinner?

Her heart and body said yes. But her head said no. So what the hell should she do?

"Hello, guys!"

Paul, who was moving to China soon, pulled up a chair next to Rick.

"I think I'll join this table with the two loveliest ladies who work at Bilton Machineries," Paul said, grinning at Jade and Lexie. "And I'm glad to see you again, Rick," Paul added.

"Thanks, Paul," Rick responded.

"Welcome to your first Halloween dinner with us, Lucas. Hope you're enjoying it so far."

"I am, Paul. Thank you," Lucas said.

"Where's your mask, Gordon?" Paul asked.

"Uh, it's over there."

Paul frowned. "Well, get it and sit here with us. There's a chair here with your name on it."

"Good idea," Gordon murmured, leaving to retrieve his mask.

Jade breathed a sigh of relief. That solved the Gordon problem. Now she just had to keep her cool beside Lucas.

More people joined their table, introducing themselves to Lucas and Rick, and allowing Jade to get her bearings back.

"You okay?" Lexie whispered.

"Yeah."

"I see why you hardly came home when you and Lucas were together. He's freakin' hot."

"Lexie!" Jade said. "You're supposed to be helping me forget that bit."

"Just remember that with that hunky look comes a bevy of girls lining up to warm his bed," Lexie said gravely.

She felt a prick in her heart. That fact hadn't stopped hurting.

"This guy next to me is hot, too," Lexie declared.

"Forget it," she said flatly. "They're birds of the same feather."

"Oh, really?" Lexie asked, a little disappointed.

"I believe so."

"Gordon's back," Lexie whispered.

Jade looked in time to see Gordon's stony face as he sat on the only chair left available—next to Lucas.

174

She sighed. Even though she hadn't told Gordon that she and Lucas had gone out in the past, Gordon correctly sensed that Lucas was a rival for her affections. She wouldn't be surprised if Gordon tried to make a competition out of it. She'd come to realise he was someone who would aggressively go after what he wanted.

Just like Lucas.

What still messed with her head was why Lucas was still persisting. She didn't want to admit it to her friends, but it impressed her. Could there be a chance that, perhaps… just maybe… he might care about her, after all?

Paul laughed, diverting Jade's attention.

"Lucas, I see you were bold enough to pick a Bilton mask," Paul said.

"Don't tell me you chose a different one," Lucas said with a grin. "I heard this was your idea. I would have thought that you, at least, would wear it."

"Well, I'm joining tonight's pantomime game and I don't want to ruin my chances of winning. You've been told Mr. Bilton's the sole judge, right?"

"Oh, these masks are for a pantomime game?" Lucas asked.

"Yes, they add to the fun of it. Your mask would be your character. You act by yourself or with a group, impromptu."

"Hey, no one told me that," Lucas said with a laugh.

"No one's forced to participate, but it'll be fun if you do. It's hilarious. Apart from the prestige, the prize is nothing to sneeze at. Mr. Bilton usually shows off his generous side during this party and the staff Christmas party."

"Right."

"So, Jade," Gordon said. "I know the winner will get a gift certificate. But what does the runner-up get?"

Jade shook her head. "You'll find out soon enough."

"Did you choose the prize for the runner-up?" Lucas asked.

"Yes," she said, nervous about what people's reaction would be to the item.

She was usually a practical, professional person when buying something work-related. But when she passed by a shop selling costume jewellery, a piece by the window just called to her. She couldn't take her eyes of it.

It was a heart-shaped necklace made from imitation ruby with a big heart-shaped hole in the middle.

It reminded her of Lucas, Ruby and Thomas—three people whose lives were turned upside down by a mystery person for reasons still unknown.

And when she stared at the hole, she felt some hope. Because even though there was an empty space in the middle, no one could deny the object was a heart—still beautiful, still vibrant. It soothed an ache within her.

She would have bought it for herself if she could have afforded it. But even though it wasn't a real ruby, it was still too expensive. She tried to save her money for Mickey's needs. It was within the budget Thomas had given her, though.

On a whim—or a rare lapse of judgement—she'd purchased it. Looking back now, the necklace was probably inappropriate as a prize for tonight's game.

She'd love to win it though. What would be her chances?

*

Jade folded her serviette and wiped the corners of her eyes. How Mr. Bilton would judge the winner of this pantomime, she had no idea. She'd been holding her sides from the antics of each and every single one of the acts, joining in the riotous laughter of everyone in the function room.

She clapped as four of her colleagues from accounting left the stage.

"Okay," said the MC. "Who's next? Raise your hand."

"Here!" Paul called out. "Come on, peeps."

"I'm not joining you up there, Paul," Lexie said with a laugh.

"Oh, come on, Rapunzel. Humour a werewolf who won't be here next year. I need your hair to climb up the stage."

Lexie rolled her eyes but stood up. "Jade?" she asked.

"I'm Sleeping Beauty," Jade said. "What can I do?"

"Just sit up there and pretend you're asleep," Paul said with a laugh.

"I'm in, too!" Gordon cried, already putting on his Dracula mask. "And I need you for my act, Jade. Please?"

With a smile, Jade rose and walked up the stage with Lexie. She wondered how Paul and Gordon would act this out, seeing they hadn't even discussed any scenario.

Would Lucas join in? She bet Thomas would be thrilled to bits to see his son wearing his mask.

Sitting next to Lucas tonight just showed her how far she was from getting over him completely. Lucas had been giving her glances that she'd chosen to ignore. But as the night wore on, she found herself wondering if he'd ever make a move on her—like bump her knee or touch her thigh.

Ugh. She was being crazy. Which proved she wasn't ready to be friends with him. He still affected her too much.

She sat on a chair in the middle of the stage and slumped, pretending to be asleep. She kept her lids slightly open, though, so she could watch the show. Lexie stood by the edge of the stage, pretending to comb her 'very, very' long hair.

Paul gripped on Lexie's invisible strands and started to climb. The audience laughed as Paul 'fell' on his ass. He got up, tried again, only to 'lose' his grip and land on his butt again. With much 'effort', Paul made it to the stage, to the audience's delight. He bowed theatrically to Lexie, who placed a finger on her lips. She was motioning for Paul to keep quiet so as not to wake Sleeping Beauty. Paul nodded, whisking Lexie away from the centre of the platform.

Gordon walked up the stage—slowly and deliberately. Then he waved his elbows up and down, as if he were flying like a bat. He swooped onto where Jade was sitting and circled her.

The audience hooted.

"Wake her up, Count!" someone called out, and others whistled in encouragement.

Jade blushed. A few of their colleagues knew Gordon was interested in her. Some probably even thought they were already dating. Argh!

She sat still, not reacting. She was supposed to be asleep. But she couldn't help but search for Lucas with her eyes. How was he reacting to this?

He wasn't at their table. Where did he go?

The audience burst into laughter.

"Go, Mr. Bilton!" someone cried.

Jade looked to her right. Lucas was climbing up the stage, Thomas Bilton's mask fixed on his face.

He sauntered towards Gordon, his hands firmly on his hips in an intimidating fashion.

Gordon clasped Jade's shoulders, as if showing Lucas he couldn't get to her.

Lucas shook his head, then with a slow deliberate movement, he pointed to Gordon then pointed to the exit.

"You're fired, Gordon," yet another workmate yelled, and there was another eruption of laughter.

"Are you gonna defy Mr. Bilton, Gordon?"

More comments were thrown about, some of them encouraging Gordon to bite Jade already then run for his life.

The MC's whistle sounded, indicating that their group's time was up.

Jade breathed a sigh of relief as the audience applauded their performance.

"Great acting, guys," Paul said as they settled back on their seats.

"Good job, Jade," Rick said with a grin. "You were very compelling up there."

Jade chuckled. "Thanks. Pretending to be asleep was such hard work."

"Glad you enjoyed it, Jade," Gordon said, giving her a smile.

She smiled back, feeling a little sorry for him. His planned act had been thwarted by Lucas.

Her heart thumped. Did Lucas mean what she thought he meant by interrupting Gordon's attempt at 'claiming' her?

She glanced at Lucas casually. He was finishing his dessert.

She took a deep breath and bumped her knee to his.

From the corner of her eye, she saw him freeze. She lifted her glass to her lips and joined in the conversation Lexie was having with Rick.

"Did you know that Rick knows my brother?" Lexie asked her in wonder.

"Really?" she asked with real surprise.

"Yes," Rick said. "We went to school together. It's a small world."

"When was the last time you saw each other?" Jade asked.

Rick's answer didn't register to Jade when she felt Lucas' hand on her thigh. Her breath caught as she tried to stifle a grin.

"Sorry, I didn't hear you," she said to Rick, flustered but happy.

"I said it's been years since Lexie's brother and I last saw each other."

"What did you say, Rick?" Lucas asked, leaning closer to Jade but looking at Rick.

Rick repeated his answers.

"Interesting connections," Lucas said, smiling at Lexie.

"I know," Lexie answered, gushing a little.

Jade narrowed her eyes. Her friend was attracted to Rick. Oh, no.

Oh, well, who was she to talk? Here she was, rubbing thighs with the man she swore she'd move on from. Mr. Fuck King, no less.

But, damn it, Lucas was wearing her defences down.

*****

Jade smiled as her boss made his way to the stage.

Everybody listened attentively as Thomas gave a speech, thanking both staff and business partners for their valued contributions throughout the year.

"I must say this year's pantomime has been the funniest I've seen so far," Thomas said. "I guess you guys must have spent a lot of time practising."

"No practice whatsoever, Mr. Bilton," Paul called out. "We're just naturally talented."

"Ladies and gentlemen," Thomas said. "Paul's not really going to China. The truth is he's joining a travelling circus to be their clown."

Jade laughed with the others, enjoying seeing this side of Thomas.

"Anyway, it's been really difficult for me to pick the runner-up and the winner. But make a decision I must, and it is final."

Everyone clapped.

"Well, we really can't go past the final act, can we?" Thomas asked. "They elicited the loudest reaction out of all the contestants."

"Woo, that's us!" Paul said.

"Before I announce the runner-up and winner, I'd like to say that Jade and Alexia did a wonderful job," Thomas said.

The audience agreed by applauding.

"And Gordon, if you didn't have a vampire mask on, I would have thought you were doing the chicken dance."

People chortled loudly.

"But it was still great acting. I was impressed."

Paul gave Gordon two thumbs up.

"So that leaves Lucas Renner and Paul Chow as the two people contesting the main prize," Thomas said. "Let me announce the winner first."

Anticipation filled the air as everyone waited in silence.

"For being willing to fall on his behind again and again, and for making us all laugh in his last Staff and Partners Halloween Dinner—in Australia, at least—the first prize goes to Paul Chow."

Cheers went up the room.

As Jade watched Paul accept his gift certificate, her heart thundered in her chest.

This meant Lucas would be getting her necklace. What would he think of it?

Paul went back to his seat and Thomas resumed the presentations.

"Lucas, Lucas, Lucas," Thomas chanted. "When I walked in here and looked at the tub with the masks, I asked why there were so many of me left behind. I was told no one wanted me. I was crushed!"

"Aww," the men exclaimed.

Jade bet most were now regretting not picking a Thomas mask.

"Well, Lucas," Thomas said. "You made me so happy when I saw you walk up the stage wearing it. And you know what? I just might give you the company as your prize, son."

Everyone laughed, taking Thomas' words as a joke.

Jade smiled at Lucas, knowing the true meaning behind the words. Lucas grinned back at her, squeezing her thigh and giving it a gentle rub. She sighed softly, feeling lightheaded.

"Come up here, Lucas. We have a prize for you."

Jade bit her lip, her breathing shallowing.

Her face burned as Lucas unwrapped the box on stage and pulled out the ruby heart. As he held it up to the audience, his gaze flickered to her, his mouth parted in… awe?

Oh, thank God. At least he didn't think it was a laughable gift.

"Something for you to give to the woman of your dreams, Lucas," Thomas said.

"Me!" came a round of shouts from different females in the room, and more laughter followed.

"That concludes our presentation," Thomas said. "Let the dancing begin."

The music started blaring as Lucas went back to his seat.

"Let's have a look," Rick said, holding his hand out for the box.

The necklace went around the table.

"Is it ruby?" Paul asked, looking at Jade.

"It looks like it but it's not. The budget Mr. Bilton gave me wouldn't buy a real ruby," she joked.

"I wouldn't have minded winning this myself," Paul said. "Except that my wife would ask why it isn't real ruby."

"With the gift certificate you got, you could get her what she wants," Rick said.

Paul sighed. "Yes, this goes to the wife. Where's yours going to, Lucas? You don't strike me as the type who'd wear it," he added teasingly.

"I have someone in mind," Lucas said, chuckling.

"I hope it's me, darling," a voice behind Jade said.

Jade turned and saw Hazel, an undeniably gorgeous woman who worked in the accounting firm used by Bilton Machineries. Did Hazel and Lucas know each other?

"Hazel!" Lucas said, clearly surprised. "What are you doing here?"

"I was invited. What are you doing here?"

"I was invited, too."

"You didn't tell me you have dealings with Bilton Machineries when we were in Japan," Hazel said.

"Didn't come up," Lucas said with a shrug.

Hazel chuckled. "Well, I expect at least one dance tonight, okay, Mr. FK? Didn't dance enough with you in Japan."

"Sure," Lucas said.

Hazel let out a throaty laugh and whispered something to Lucas. Lucas grinned, whispering something back to Hazel. Hazel nodded, touching Lucas' biceps, before sauntering off.

Jade stared at Hazel.

Japan? Didn't dance enough?

Mr. FK?

And why the hell did Lucas respond to Hazel's flirtations *right in front of her?*

"I'm going to the bathroom," she said to Lexie.

Lexie read her expression. "I'm going with you."

Jade kept a bright smile pasted on her face as she and Lexie made their way to the ladies'. When they were out of the function room, Jade let it drop.

"I'm so stupid, Lex," she said.

"Why?"

"Didn't you hear what Hazel said? She called him Mr. FK. That means Mr. Fuck King. They know each other and were in Japan together. And they *danced* while they were there!" she said with distaste. "Then he let her whisper in his ear. *When I was looking!*"

Lexie sighed. "I knew you were weakening back there. Your eyes went soft and you started smiling at him sweetly."

"I already said I'm so stupid."

"Well, snap out of it."

"I am," Jade said quietly. "It won't happen again."

CHAPTER EIGHTEEN

Lucas sat on his chair while the others went to the dance floor, or mingled. He was waiting for Jade. By the looks of it he was in trouble again.

He let out a huge sigh. Just when he was getting somewhere with Jade, Hazel had to appear and flirt with him. Damn it.

Hazel was a stunning woman with a mischievous streak that could turn devious. Used to getting her way because of her looks, Hazel would simply turn up her flirtations rather than retreat when faced with competition.

He'd been so surprised that Hazel was here. The last time they bumped into each other was in Japan, when she'd gone to watch the Formula One race.

If he hadn't acknowledged Hazel the way he did, Hazel would just have cranked up her 'charm' full blast. He'd wanted to avoid the attention that would generate. He'd thought it was a smart move at the time.

But nope, he was clearly wrong. He saw Jade's reaction, and before he could explain, she'd dragged Lexie with her to go outside—to the ladies', presumably.

Hell, hell, hell.

He felt a hand on his shoulder. It was Thomas, who sat down on Jade's vacant seat.

"Nice speech up there, sir," he said, smiling warmly at his father.

"Thank you. And I'm really glad you're getting to meet our staff and business partners. This is a great way to get to know them."

Lucas chuckled. "I haven't told you my decision yet," he said, glancing around. No one seemed to be eavesdropping. He guessed no one would dare anyway.

"Don't tell me it's anything other than you joining the company!" Thomas said. "It's better if you start early, Lucas, while I've got plenty of years left to help prepare you for when you head it in the future."

"I was thinking of quitting Formula One even before we met. It's to join my friend Connor in his business. Part of my hesitation is that I've promised him that when I stop touring, we'll be partners and build a strong, nationwide chain of luxury car service centres."

"It had crossed my mind that that's your issue, Lucas. There's nothing stopping you from being involved in your friend's business. The only question is how much time you want to give to that and to Bilton Machineries. You can most definitely support his business as an advisor or investor, while still working at our company full time."

That option sounded attractive to Lucas. He'd love to work with Connor, but more and more he was finding his interest leaning towards Bilton Machineries. "I'll speak with Connor," he said. "Then I'll give you my decision in the next couple of days."

Thomas nodded, pleased, before his demeanour turned serious. "We need to talk about other developments. The investigators just called. They think they know the man responsible."

Lucas wandered the room, looking for Jade. He hadn't seen her since she left with Lexie. Surely she hadn't gone home?

He wanted to find her before he had to go himself. He and Thomas didn't want to wait until tomorrow to discuss the new information dug up by the investigators. They were very close to finding out who'd been trying to sabotage their lives.

From the other end of the room, Lucas noticed Thomas' driver motion to him. He nodded. It was time to leave.

With a big exhale and a heavy heart, he walked towards the exit.

He'd talk to Jade tomorrow—if she'd pick up his call. How would he get her to listen?

*****

Lucas placed his hand on his father's shoulder as Thomas stared at the investigator in shock.

"Are you sure?" Thomas asked, anger and incredulity in his tone. "This is an extremely serious accusation."

"We went over everything multiple times before we rang you, sir. We wanted to be absolutely sure."

Lucas glanced at Thomas' ashen face, before facing the investigator. "I guess his primary motive is to make sure I don't make a claim for my father's fortune."

"It would appear so, sir."

"Is... does... what about Diana?" Thomas asked shakily.

"She doesn't appear to be involved, sir. In fact, evidence suggests she was kept in the dark, too."

Thomas breathed a sigh of relief. "I will talk to him," he said in a stronger voice. "I want all your documentary evidence so he can't explain his way out of it."

"I'm going with you," Lucas said.

"Lucas," Thomas said. "I'd like this first confrontation to be between him and me only. He is my father-in-law. You can have your day with him after."

Lucas hesitated, then nodded. While Diana's father also messed up with his and Ruby's lives, this was much more personal for Thomas.

"I still can't believe it," Thomas said softly. "But I think I know why he went to such great lengths to keep us apart, Lucas."

"To protect Diana and his family's reputation?" Lucas guessed. Diana's father most probably didn't want the world to know that his son-in-law had fathered a child with an escort while engaged to his daughter.

"Yes. For sure. But that's not all. He's also trying to protect his family's lifestyle."

"What do you mean?" Lucas asked.

"Not long after he pulled his money from Bilton Machineries, he invested heavily in a failed venture. He almost went bankrupt, and was weeks from shutting down his business. That broke him.

"Around that time, I became successful in securing the support of investors to plug in the financial hole. I decided to help him keep his business afloat as my

189

way of making amends for my own actions. That kept the impression that he wasn't in any financial trouble. My father-in-law is a very proud man and would have avoided anything that cast his name in a negative light."

"But to do what he did…" Lucas said. "It just seems so unbelievably cruel."

"Some people can't handle heavy pressure, Lucas. They don't have the fortitude, especially if it involves falling from great heights. I believe my father-in-law is such a man. And I think that he might have compensated for that kind of failure by controlling what he could. In this case, it was your mother when she was at her most vulnerable. And once he started, well, I suppose he thought he couldn't stop or else he'd be found out."

"Now he's been found out," Lucas murmured.

"Yes. He has been. We're close to sorting this out, son," Thomas said, smiling at him with sad, sad eyes.

Lucas embraced his father and gave him whatever comfort he could. Thomas had found him, only to lose another family member. He hoped Thomas and Diana could weather this storm.

*****

Lucas waited until someone opened the front door of Jade's apartment building before slipping in. He doubted that Jade would let him in if he buzzed. He'd tried to ring her all morning and she didn't answer.

He went up her floor and knocked on the door, making sure that the three dozen red roses he was carrying covered his face from the peephole.

190

The door opened and he breathed a little sigh of relief. Unfortunately, it was Cassie.

"Hi," Cassie said warily.

"Hi, Cassie. Is Jade in please?"

"No. She's at her brother's."

Disappointment hit him. "Could you tell me the address?"

Cassie huffed. "No. Sorry."

"Please, Cassie. I need to talk to her."

"Why?" Cassie said, her voice challenging.

He inhaled deeply. "I need to explain a few things to her."

"Lucas, she's moving on. Please respect her decision."

No. He couldn't accept that. "If she gives me a chance to explain, I'll respect whatever decision she makes after that."

"What made you change your mind, Lucas? Why did you break up with her? Why did you tell her you're not into relationships and tell her you've—what was it you said—gone as far as you can?"

"That was a mistake, Cassie," he said, pleading.

Cassie shook her head. "Sorry, Lucas. Anyway, it's not me you have to convince. And she's not home."

"Won't you tell me Jerry's address?"

"No. You can ask Jade yourself."

"But she won't answer my calls!"

"Tough, then," Cassie said, closing the door.

"Wait, Cassie. Could you please give these flowers to Jade?"

"I'd rather not, Lucas," she said, then shut the door on his face.

He groaned silently. What else could he do? Cassie wouldn't help, and he didn't want to pile up a problem on his dad when Thomas had his own personal issues to deal with.

He walked away, dejected.

*****

"Hey, bro! Long time, no see. And you brought me roses!"

"Yeah," Lucas said with a smirk, handing the bouquet to Connor. "I thought you might like them."

Connor frowned, staring at the flowers with suspicion. "What? Are these really for me?"

"They were supposed to be for Jade," he said with a sigh. "You could give them to Amanda if you want."

"Thanks. She'd love them. But why did you get flowers for Jade?" Connor asked as he put the bouquet down on a table.

"To say I'm sorry. But she wouldn't even see me."

"Hey, I thought we'd established that Jade is Thomas' willing pawn?"

"Rick hasn't told you?"

"Last time I spoke to Rick was at Greg's party. We've all been busy, I guess."

Lucas updated Connor with all the recent developments.

"Oh," Connor said, sitting on a chair with a dismayed look on his face.

"What?"

"At the party... Marilyn came around... she mentioned your title. Jade heard."

Lucas felt heat rise to his neck and face. "Mr. Fuck King? Did Marilyn tell Jade what it means?"

"I kinda told her because she asked me. At the time, I thought she was scheming with Thomas so I didn't think it would matter. Actually, I was thinking that at least she'd see that she didn't have you under her thumb."

Lucas' chest heaved.

"Sorry, dude," Connor said softly.

He nodded, raking his hair. "Hazel was at the Bilton Halloween party," he said to Connor.

"Bombshell Hazel?" Connor said, an eyebrow lifting.

"Yes. The accounting firm she works for is Bilton Machineries' accountants. She called me Mr. FK then, and flirted with me. In front of Jade."

"Oh."

He rubbed his face harshly. "Jade probably has all sorts of pictures running through her mind," he said. Sadly, most of them would probably be accurate. But he hadn't been acting like Mr. Fuck King since that first time they'd made out on her couch. Heck, that wasn't even true. He hadn't been with any other woman since he first carried flowers for her to the Bilton Machineries building.

"What do I do now?" he asked Connor.

"Plead, beg, walk on broken glass…" Connor said quietly. "If she's really the one, Lucas, you'll find yourself wanting to do everything to get her back."

Lucas paused, taking in Connor's words. He didn't need long at all to think about it.

"She's the one, Connor."

Connor grinned. "Who'll be Mr. Fuck King now?"

"Can't think of anyone worthy enough of the title, bro," he joked. "Maybe we retire it. So in its history, there were only two—you and me."

"Suits me," Connor said with a grin.

"Now I have to get some broken glass," Lucas murmured.

"It might help if you walk on it on your knees," Connor said, his lips twitching.

"Anything else?" he asked wryly.

Connor sighed, his demeanour turning serious. "Yeah. Good luck. I mean that."

He smiled his thanks. "By the way, Connor, about being business partners..."

Connor clasped his shoulder. "I know your future's at Bilton Machineries, Lucas. It's cool."

"Thanks, bro. I'm still keen to do something with you, not just in the way we've originally discussed."

"That would be great."

"Well, I better head back to Jade's and wait for her to come home."

*****

Lucas sat by the window of the coffee shop at the corner of Jade's street. Thankfully, Cassie had caved and told him that Jade should be back at around five o'clock.

In was only four, but he didn't want to go somewhere else only to come back. So he'd hang around here at the café while he waited.

His phone rang. The screen indicated No Caller ID, which meant it was most probably his mother, who insisted on keeping her privacy.

194

"Lucas Renner," he answered.

"Hello, darling. I went grocery shopping today and there were fresh food items on sale so I got you some. Do you want to come and get them tonight?"

He smiled. He'd given up trying to stop his mother from buying groceries for him. Nothing he'd done had been effective.

"Thanks, Mum. I'm not sure if I can tonight. Can I let you know later?"

"Sure. Just let me know when."

"I will. Thanks, Mum."

He hung up and noticed the server, who was cleaning up the table next to his, looking at him.

"Hi," the lady said, coming over and smiling. She was quite pretty. Not as attractive as Jade, though.

"Hi."

"Did I hear you say you're Lucas Renner?" she asked.

"Yes," he answered with surprise.

"And do you know Jade and Cassie, who live in an apartment not far from here?"

"Yes."

The woman chuckled, as if amused by that fact. "Jade's right. You're my kind of hunk."

He raised his eyebrows. "Excuse me?"

"I'm Penelope," she said with a sultry smile, her eyelashes batting.

"Hi, Penelope," he said warily, not at all sure why this woman seemed to be flirting with him.

"Jade and Cassie were here a few days ago, and I happened to tell them that I'm single again and ready for my next adventure. Jade mentioned that she knew someone who was my perfect match, and his name's Lucas Renner."

"What?" he asked, shocked.

"I already noticed you when you came through the door. Imagine my surprise when I heard you say your name," Penelope said, twirling a strand of hair.

Lucas stared at Penelope in disbelief. Jade had told Penelope that he was this woman's perfect match? Why the hell would Jade do that?

"Don't look so shocked," Penelope said with a giggle. "I've set Jade up on a blind date before. We girls just exchange favours."

"And Jade was trying to set us up?"

"Unfortunately, we didn't get to chat for too long because it was busy when they were here. And Gordon arrived then too, so we kinda stopped our girl talk."

"Gordon?" he asked weakly.

"Yes. I think he's Jade's new boyfriend. Anyway…" Penelope took out a pad and pen from her apron pocket and scribbled something. "Here's my number. I trust Jade's instincts that the two of us might be perfect for each other." She gave him a playful wink as she placed the sheet of paper on the table, then sashayed off.

Lucas slumped on his seat as he stared incredulously at Penelope. Was that why Jade didn't want to talk to him? Because she simply had stopped being interested?

He glanced at Penelope's phone number and his heart felt like it was being wrung dry by merciless hands.

Jade didn't want him anymore. She'd discarded him. Not only was she ignoring him, not only was she going out with Gordon, but she'd also literally given him away to another woman.

His eyes stung. He'd thought he was someone who knew the pain of rejection. But this was worse than anything he'd ever felt.

For the first time in his life, he'd fallen in love. For the first time, he was ready for commitment. But the woman he loved didn't want him.

She'd given him away.

He pulled out his wallet, placed money on the table, and hurried to the exit. He didn't want anyone to see that his eyes were swimming in tears.

CHAPTER NINETEEN

"Hi, Cass," Jade called out as she entered the apartment.

"Hey, Jade," Cassie replied. "Did you see Lucas downstairs? He said he was going to wait for you to come home."

"No," she said with a frown, heading for the kitchen where Cassie was.

"Oh. Maybe he had to go. He buzzed twice today, you know. The first time, he had this massive bouquet of red roses. But I didn't take it because you told me not to entertain him at all. Then he came back a couple of hours later, pleading with me to tell him when you'll be back. I felt so sorry for him, so I said you'll be home by five."

Jade checked the time. It was half past five. Why didn't she come home earlier?

"You're softening, aren't you?" Cassie asked gently.

"I think I should at least listen to him, Cass. He's been trying so hard."

"It's your choice, Jade."

"I'm just scared," she whispered.

"I know," Cassie said soothingly. "His reputation is not exactly the type that you associate with faithfulness and commitment."

"No. But I love him, Cass," she blurted out.

"Oh, honey," Cassie said, hugging her.

"I don't know what to do."

"You *know* what you want to do. You just don't know if what you want will get you hurt."

Jade took a deep breath, her mind clearing suddenly. "You're right. And you know what? Stuff fear. People like Lucas do change. His friend Connor is an example. What if he wants to change for me? I don't want to throw away our opportunity."

Cassie nodded her agreement.

"Thank you," she said, hugging her best friend before retrieving her phone to call Lucas. To her relief, he answered.

"Jade."

"Hi," she said, a little breathless. "Cassie said you were here earlier."

"Yes."

"I'm sorry I missed you. I'm home now," she said with a tinge of hope.

There was a long silence.

"So what do you want to do now, Jade?"

She frowned at the flatness of his tone. "I thought you wanted to talk."

"I did," he said in the same bleak voice. "But I had coffee at that café at the corner of your street while I waited for you. I already got my answer there."

"What do you mean, Lucas?"

She heard his ragged sigh.

"I get the picture, Jade. I get it," he said with a shaky voice. "I agree there's no need for us to have a further conversation. Take care of yourself." Then he hung up.

Jade stared at her phone in disbelief.

"What did he say?" Cassie asked.

"He sounded upset," she said, bewildered. "He said he got his answer at the corner café and there was no need for us to talk anymore."

"Huh?"

Realisation hit Jade. "Do you think Penelope talked to him?"

Cassie covered her mouth. "Oh no. Penelope would be all over someone like Lucas. And she honestly didn't get that you were being sarcastic when you said that she and Lucas were the perfect match."

Jade's eyes watered. "Lucas thinks I don't want him anymore." She turned and headed for the door. "I'll see you later, Cass. I need to see him."

*****

"I'm sorry, Jade, but my son can be a very stubborn man. And he's not used to expressing his feelings," Ruby said apologetically. "He doesn't want to talk to me either. He keeps giving excuses not to see me."

Jade sniffed. "I don't know what else to do, Ruby. If even you can't make him talk to me, what other options do I have?"

"He's afraid," Ruby said, patting her hand. "He's never had his heart broken before. You yourself would know that when you're still raw and hurting, you want to retreat from the source of pain."

"But I want to fix things," she whispered. "Whatever Penelope said to him wasn't the truth. I was hurt after learning about his reputation. I was being sarcastic when I suggested that Lucas was Penelope's type because she's a playgirl and he's..."

"I know, darling. But remember that he's also experiencing emotional upheaval and stress from the matters involving Thomas and Thomas' father-in-law. Things might be a bit too much for Lucas at this point. Give him some time. He'll come around."

She sniffed again, hoping Ruby was right.

"Apart from this, is everything okay with you?" Ruby asked.

She smiled guiltily. She'd been so focused on her own issues that she'd forgotten to check how Ruby was coping.

"I'm fine, thank you," she answered. "More importantly, how are you?"

"Good, thank you. It's actually funny how I more or less feel the same—just lighter. I mean, something I've lived with and believed in for thirty years turned out to be wrong. And here I am, still running my shop as per usual," Ruby said with a smile.

"I'm glad things have worked out for all three of you, Ruby."

"Thank you, Jade. And I hope that things work out for you and Lucas, too. I'll do my best to help."

"Thank you."

*****

"Here they are, Mr. Bilton," Jade said, handing over the documents her boss had asked her to collate.

"Thank you, Jade."

Jade noticed the bags under her boss's eyes and her heart went to him.

It humbled her that Thomas had seen fit to share with her the news regarding his father-in-law. She couldn't believe it, but she was glad they'd now resolved the matter.

Diana's father had broken down and fully confessed when Lucas came with Thomas for another round of confrontation. The elderly man had to be taken to hospital for a minor heart attack after his admission of guilt, but fortunately, he'd pull through.

Diana was still in shock, though, and Thomas had to look after her on top of everything else.

It was the one big reason why she hadn't asked Thomas about Lucas. She didn't want to add to the stress Thomas was already under.

But she wished she could come up with other options to reach Lucas. He was avoiding her just like she used to avoid him. Only in Lucas' case, it was worse. He seemed to have put her number on a permanent block on his phone. She didn't do that to him!

"Jade," Thomas called as she was on her way out of his office.

"Sir?"

"I need to make an important phone call now. If Lucas arrives before I'm done, could you tell him I'll meet him at the restaurant where we're having lunch?"

"Yes, sir," she said, a smile blossoming on her face. She hoped Thomas would stay on the phone for a long time.

She was typing something when she saw Lucas approach, and her heart immediately raced.

"Hi, Jade," he said with a small smile.

"Hi," she responded, but Lucas was already on his way to his father's office. He didn't want to stop to talk to her.

"Lucas, wait," she called out.

Fortunately, he turned around.

"Mr. Bilton's still on the phone."

Lucas looked disappointed. "Okay. Could you tell him I'll meet him at the restaurant? I'll go there now."

Her heart dropped to the floor. "I've been trying to call you," she said desperately.

"Were you?" he asked innocently. "Sorry. I've been busy."

"Lucas... I know that Penelope said things—"

"Hey, forget about that," he interrupted with a dismissive wave of his hand. "It's all cool."

"But it's not," she whispered, stopping when Ann, the receptionist, passed by to hand her something.

"You've blocked my calls and messages," she whispered when Ann was out of earshot.

"Oh, yeah," he said lightly. "It was just my reaction on the day. Don't worry about it."

"So will you unblock me and talk to me?"

"I'm talking to you now, am I not?" he said with a grin that didn't reach his eyes. "And I won't be around for a while anyway. I'll be visiting different branches interstate and overseas, staying in each for a few weeks to months to learn the business. I'll be away for a long time."

"No," she whispered, but Lucas was already on his way to the lifts.

She stood up to run after him, but her office phone rang. Argh!

"Mr. Bilton's office, Jade speaking," she answered in her professional voice.

"Hi, Jade. It's Rick."

"Hi, Rick. How are you?"

"Well, thanks. I'm just calling to see if Mr. Bilton received the invitation for our Christmas party? My PA is on leave and I have a temp helping out. Unfortunately, she stuffed some of the invitations in the wrong envelope."

"I don't remember seeing it arrive. When was it sent?"

Rick sighed. "Last week. It should be there by now if it was addressed correctly. Thanks anyway. I'll get her to redo it again."

"Okay. Thanks, Rick."

Jade hung up and an idea popped into her head. Perhaps Rick could be a way to get Lucas to talk to her?

*****

Jade stared at herself in the mirror. She wasn't a prude, but this new one-piece swimsuit with a deep V-neck she was wearing was making her blush. It was by far the sexiest thing she'd ever worn.

"If Lucas' eyes don't fall out of their sockets when he sees you in that, then definitely move on to the next guy," Erin said.

"I agree," said Cassie. "Anyone who doesn't drool over you today is blind—man or woman."

She laughed. "Oh, girls. You sure know how to boost my ego."

Erin grinned. "What are best friends for? But for the record, we mean every word. Don't we, Cass?"

"Absolutely," Cass said.

"Well, you girls look just as hot," Jade said, casting her glance at her friends, who were wearing less revealing, but equally sexy, swimsuits.

The door clicked and Lexie came bounding in the hotel room they'd booked for the day. "Wow, Jade! Look at you!"

"Gosh, you guys are really making me nervous," Jade said.

Lexie laughed. "Let me get changed and we can go."

Jade took a deep breath, praying that this day would end the way she hoped.

Brad, Lexie's older brother, was celebrating his thirtieth birthday. He'd reserved several cabanas for the afternoon on the rooftop pool bar of one of Sydney's entertainment venues. While Brad had only planned to invite family and close friends, Lexie had managed to convince Brad to also invite his old chum from school—Rick. Then Lexie had asked Rick to take Lucas as his plus one.

"What if he doesn't turn up?" Jade asked, looking at her friends' reflection in the mirror.

"Rick has RSVP'd for both himself and Lucas. I'm sure Lucas is coming," Lexie said from the bathroom.

"I just hope he doesn't learn that Rick's friend Brad is your brother, Lex. He'd get suspicious and pull out."

"He'll turn up," Lexie said. "He has no clue you'll be here. I asked Rick to make sure of that."

"Quit worrying, Jade," Cassie said. "You're supposed to be the seductive siren today. A worried face doesn't go with the picture. Now why don't you practice your sexy look? Pretend you're in front of Lucas."

Jade chuckled and posed in front of the mirror, pouting sultrily.

"Great!" Lexie said, coming out of the bathroom. "Now, ladies, put on your wrap-around dresses and let's go. The party's already starting."

"Okay," Jade said with quiet determination.

She had no idea what she was going to say to Lucas today. But she planned to chat him up and flirt with him, whether he liked it or not. And hopefully convince him to take her home.

*****

Jade's breath caught in her throat when she spotted Lucas in one of the cabanas by the pool. He was chatting to Brad and Rick, looking relaxed and oh, so handsome.

Two women occupying a cabana on the other side of the pool were already eyeing the guys, giggling and taking off their dresses to reveal their bikinis underneath.

Whoa. Talk about skimpy. Now Jade wondered if her one-piece would be adequate for keeping Lucas' attention.

She walked towards the guys, her heart hammering in her chest. Lucas could very well ignore her all afternoon, but she'd psyched herself not to give up until he literally told her to leave him alone. Even then, she might not obey, knowing he was acting from a place of hurt. Since she'd caused that hurt, she hoped to heal it, too—if he'd let her.

"Hello, girls," Brad said, spotting them approach.

Lucas and Rick turned around, and Jade noticed that Lucas wasn't surprised to see her. Perhaps he'd already learned that Brad was Lexie's brother. Well, shouldn't he be flattered that she was going out of her way to get his attention?

"Happy birthday, Brad," Erin said.

While the other girls greeted the birthday boy, Jade smiled at Lucas. "Hi," she said.

"Hi," he said with a small smile.

"Glad to see you here," she said a little breathlessly.

"Yeah, you, too," he responded before bringing his attention to the girls greeting Brad.

"I've been wanting to talk to you about your conversation with Penelope," she said tentatively.

"Come on, Jade. We're at a party," Lucas responded, not even looking at her. "This isn't the time."

She repressed a sigh. He was hiding his hurt. And still mad at her.

A cocktail waitress came with a tray of drinks. Jade was picking one when a small beach ball came flying their way and hit Lucas' leg.

"Oops, sorry," said one of the women in skimpy bikini. She gave Lucas a smile while biting her bottom lip. No prizes for guessing her level of interest in Lucas.

"No worries," Lucas said with a smile. He picked up the ball and walked to the edge the pool to hand it to Miss Obvious.

"Thank you. I'm Sandra, by the way."

Miss Obvious was fast. And annoying.

"I'm Lucas."

"Thank you, Lucas," Sandra said, giving Lucas another winning smile before returning to her friend.

When Lucas turned back to their group, he was smiling. And ignored Jade.

Ouch.

It wasn't even five minutes into the party and Jade was already starting to feel glum.

She felt a hand on her arm. It was Lexie, smiling at her encouragingly.

Right. Plenty of time left. She couldn't let a small hiccup ruin her plans.

*

"You all right?" Cassie whispered.

She nodded. It had been a couple of hours and still no indication of Lucas thawing. Sure, he'd chatted with her, even sounded friendly, but only to answer her questions. There was no sign of him wanting to flirt back no matter how high she turned up the flirt dial.

It was depressing.

"I'm going into the water," she said.

Miss Sandra Obvious and her friend were back in their cabana, munching on some kebabs. This would be a good time to show off her swimsuit without those two bombshells to compete with.

She took off her wrap-around dress and laid it on a bench with her towel. Then she walked gracefully to the pool steps and went into the water. She glanced back to see if Lucas had noticed.

Yes! He was looking at her. But in the next instant, he turned to resume chatting with the other guests.

She huffed. What should she make of that?

With a sigh, she settled herself on a step, the water reaching to the tops of her breasts. She tried to relax to let new ideas in. Perhaps she needed to be more aggressive. But how?

A few minutes later, there was loud splashing near her. Three of Brad's friends had jumped into the pool.

"The water's nice, guys," one of them said to their group.

Soon, some of Brad's other guests had joined them in the pool.

Including Lucas.

She swooned as she stared at his muscular chest. She missed seeing him naked.

Putting on an impish smile, she waded to where he was and playfully splashed him.

"Hey," he said, wiping the water off his face.

She splashed him again, grinning and hoping he'd reciprocate in kind.

"Stop it, Jade," he said, his smile forced. He glanced around as if to find an escape.

She swallowed her hurt. Hadn't she been obvious enough? She'd been making a fool of herself all afternoon. Couldn't he tell she was trying so hard?

Tears rushed to her eyes and threatened to fall. She swam away before anyone could see.

And no, Lucas didn't follow.

When she climbed out of the pool, she heard Sandra call Lucas. Jade didn't look to see how he responded to Sandra. Her heart couldn't take any more today. It needed a rest.

She walked back to the cabana, disheartened.

CHAPTER TWENTY

Lucas bit his tongue to distract him from the pain in his chest as he watched Jade swim away. He'd been surprised by the way she'd flirted with him today, and for a while there, hope had flared.

But he squashed it. She was just being friendly, wanting to make sure they were fine with each other.

Wasn't she with Gordon now? And worst of all, hadn't she tried to give him away to her friend Penelope?

That fact still cut him like nothing ever had.

He wasn't ready to be friends with her. He didn't know when he would be—*if* he ever would be.

"Hi, Lucas!"

Lucas turned just as Sandra came into the water beside him.

"Which of your buddies is having a party?" she asked.

"Brad. That guy over there," he said, pointing to the man he'd just met today. He still couldn't believe Rick had conned him into coming to Lexie's brother's birthday. He hadn't had a chance to confront his friend on it, but he bet Rick—and Ruby and Thomas—just wanted him and Jade to be comfortable around each other. But couldn't they see he needed some time before he could get there?

"Hey, you must work out a lot," Sandra said, touching his arm. The full-on flirtation had started.

Lucas was mildly amused, but mostly disinterested. He wondered how he could get rid of Sandra.

"Lucas," Rick called. "Can I borrow you for a minute?"

Relieved, Lucas excused himself and got out of the pool to follow Rick in a quiet corner.

"What are you doing?" Rick demanded.

"What do you mean?"

"You're flirting with that woman and ignoring Jade."

"I'm not flirting with Sandra and I'm not ignoring Jade," he declared.

"Oh? So when you don't respond to Jade trying to chat you up all afternoon, that's not ignoring her?"

He gulped. "I can't, Rick."

"You can't what?"

"I can't be friends with her."

"Who says she wants to be friends?" Rick asked with disbelief.

"That's all she wants. She tried to give me away," he answered, not attempting to hide his hurt.

"No, she didn't," Rick said with exasperation. "You dumped her and told her you don't do relationships. Then she found out you're called Mr. Fuck King. When she mentioned that in passing to that Penelope woman, it was because she was hurt and frustrated. She was being sarcastic because Penelope's a player and you're the same."

"Was," Lucas interrupted.

"What?"

"I *was* a player. I haven't been for a while now," he said softly.

Rick smirked, shaking his head. "Jade didn't give you away to anyone at all, Lucas. Obviously, Penelope took her words seriously even though Jade never meant for her to."

Lucas stared at Rick.

"The two of you should just talk and lay everything out," Rick continued. "Right now you're doing nothing but hurting each other and yourselves."

"I've never heard you speak like this, bro," he said.

Rick shrugged. "Lexie was very impassioned when she told me Jade's side of the story. I think Lexie's emotions about the matter have rubbed off on me."

"So it was Lexie's idea for you to take me to Brad's party so Jade and I could talk?"

Rick rolled his eyes. "No. This was all Jade's idea. You keep rebuffing her, so she asked Lexie to plead with Brad to invite you and me. Didn't you notice this was supposed to be family and close friends only? I haven't seen Brad in years, but we're here."

Lucas' gaze went to the cabana, looking for Jade, his heart thundering in his chest.

She wasn't there.

"I saw her leave with Cassie," Rick said softly. "I think she was in tears."

Lucas' own eyes moistened. "Thanks, bro. And could you tell Brad I said thank you? I have to find Jade."

*****

213

Lucas knocked on the door of the girls' hotel room. Lexie and Erin had told him where Cassie had taken Jade, but not before giving him a verbal serve for his hurtful behaviour.

He'd grinned at them, not minding their words at all. Jade wanted him back.

Cassie opened the door.

"Hi, Cassie. May I come in, please?"

"Why?"

He inhaled deeply. Cassie seemed to like interrogating him at the door.

"Let him in, Cass," Jade said from the inside, sounding sniffly.

With a little reluctance, Cassie motioned for him to walk in.

"You can rejoin the others at the party, Cass," Jade said, staring at Lucas from her sitting position on the bed. Her eyes were red and puffy.

His heart pinched and he walked towards her.

"Call us if you need us," Cassie said softly before leaving the room.

"Jade," he said, sitting next to her on the bed. "I'm so sorry, baby."

Her eyes watered again and he cupped her face. His heart compressed at seeing her distress, but at the same time he felt it start to mend.

"I thought you were just trying to be friends," he said, running his thumbs on her cheeks. "And I just couldn't handle that. I didn't mean to hurt you."

"I'm sorry, too. I never meant for Penelope to take me seriously. And I shouldn't have ignored your earlier pleas for us to talk."

"I can see why you felt you had to stay away from me. I don't exactly have the reputation of a saint," he said dryly. "I'm sorry I kept it from you. I was afraid you'd never want to see me again if you knew."

"Are you still Mr. Fuck King?"

"No, baby. That title isn't for me anymore," he said, unable to stop caressing her face. "I haven't been with anyone else since I met you."

Jade smiled. "Really?"

"Yes, really. In fact, I haven't had sex since I was last with you. And that was such a long time ago now," he said with a grin. "I don't think I've ever gone without sex for *that* long."

She giggled. "You must have incredible pent-up sexual energy seeking for release, then."

"That I do. But you know what feels like bursting inside me more than anything?" he asked, his voice breaking.

Jade sniffed, a tear running down her cheek. "This?" she whispered as she placed her hand right above his heart.

He nodded, looking deep into her eyes. "I love you, Jade." He pressed her hand on his chest so she could feel how hard and fast his heart was beating. "Only you can do this to me. I love you so much."

Jade sobbed softly. "I love you, too, Lucas."

With a shaky, happy smile he kissed her.

Jade's arms curved around his neck and she pulled him down on the bed with her.

"Who's taking the title Mr. Fuck King now?" Jade asked against his lips.

"No one," he answered, his hand roaming her body.

"Can you keep the title?"

He reared to look at her in surprise. "Why?"

She grinned. "I kinda like the idea of having Mr. Fuck King all to myself."

He laughed. "I'm sure no one would mind. Now, do you want Mr. Fuck King to do his thing?" he murmured, untying her robe.

"Mm. Yes, please," Jade responded, shifting to help him get her naked.

"I hope your friends don't interrupt us," he said, eagerly stripping his own clothes off.

"Oh, I better text them." Jade got off the bed to retrieve her phone from her bag.

He watched her. Or rather, he devoured her with his eyes. He missed her so damn much and it had been so long.

His hand went to his burgeoning erection, unable to resist giving himself a few strokes as he gawked at his naked girlfriend while she tapped a message on her phone.

"Maybe tell them to get another room so we can have this one to ourselves all night," he suggested.

Jade snickered and glanced at him. Her mouth dropped open as she watched him touch himself, her eyes taking on a dreamy look.

"Send that message already, babe," he implored. "I'd really prefer you to be doing this."

Jade's lips tugged into that sultry-shy smile he loved seeing. "Yes, I think I'll ask them to get themselves another room," she said, tapping for a few more seconds and dropping her phone on the table.

Then she slowly made her way towards the bed, running her heated eyes on his body. His cock jerked.

"See? I missed you so much, honey," he said, grinning at her and loving the way she made him burn by just a look.

Jade straddled his thighs. "So you want me to do this?" she asked, prying his hand from his hardness and replacing it with hers.

He moaned his answer.

"Like this?" Jade whispered, tugging him just like she knew he wanted.

"Jade…" he whispered. He sat up so they were nose to nose, and he ran his hand up her breast. He flicked an already excited nipple with his thumb.

She arched her back to him.

"Did you miss me?" he whispered, kissing her neck while her hand continued to pleasure him.

"So much," she answered.

"Me, too." He dipped his head to take a rosy bud in his mouth.

Jade gasped. "I missed that."

"Glad to know, sweetheart," he murmured before he paid attention to the other one.

Jade ran her thumb on the tip of his cock, spreading the wetness that had formed there.

"Honey," he cried.

To his surprise, Jade pushed him back so he was lying on the bed.

"Do you want something else other than my hand?" she asked softly.

"What do you have in mind?" he croaked, loving this game.

"Well, there are two things I can think of, but I'll save the best for last. So for now, you can have this." She bent down and took him in her mouth.

"Ahh, babe… yes," he gasped, throwing his head back on the pillow in sheer pleasure.

"Hmm. I missed doing this," Jade said, licking his length while both hands continued to caress.

He grinned as he moaned. She was incredible.

He propped himself on his elbows and watched her, loving what she was doing with her mouth. She was so damn beautiful. But she couldn't have all the fun.

Sitting up, he gently pushed her head away. "My turn," he said.

Jade smiled excitedly and got on her back.

He chuckled, his heart warmed by her eagerness, just as his body heated up a few more degrees. Nothing turned him on more than knowing Jade was aroused and craving for his touch.

"Come," he said, taking her hand and pulling her off the bed.

"Where?" she asked in surprise.

He led her to the bathroom, but only to take a clean towel. Then he guided her to a sofa with a thick, chunky back rest that was against the window. He laid the towel on the top of the back rest and patted.

"Sit here."

She raised her eyebrows and peered outside.

"No one will see us unless they have binoculars," he said.

Jade's lips curved and she stepped on the sofa to perch herself on top of the back rest, her feet on the seat.

"Now what?" she asked impishly.

"Now what do you want me to do?" he asked seductively.

She blushed, then opened her legs.

He grinned, heart pounding. Jade was the only woman who'd ever made him feel like his heart was just as excited as his dick during sex.

He'd never understood the meaning of intimate connection before her, because he'd never felt it. Only Jade had breached the physical barrier to take him to an altogether different level. Sex with her was... special. Incredibly special.

"Are you just gonna stand there?" she asked. "Or did you want to watch me?"

She put her hand between her legs.

He moaned and strode to the sofa. Then he knelt in front of her.

"Yes, I want to watch," he said, running his hands on her thighs.

Jade gulped, pinking.

"Show me, baby," he said, giving her leg a swift kiss. "I don't want there to be any embarrassment between us. I love you."

She smiled and opened her legs wider. Then she wet her fingers with her juices before rubbing her nub, gasping as she did so.

His breathing shallowed, his tongue poking out of his mouth as he watched the most erotic thing he'd ever seen. Oh, other women had done this in front of him. But this was *his* Jade.

Ah, he simply couldn't fathom how special she was compared to all the others. It still blew his mind.

And now he wanted to do more than watch.

"Keep rubbing, baby," he murmured as he licked around the lips before pushing his tongue into her slit.

Jade moaned loudly, taking her finger off her nub and raking his hair with both hands.

He was glad to fully take over and set his tongue loose on her clit.

"Lucas!"

With his mouth not missing a beat, he reached up to tweak her nipples.

"Oh God," Jade cried, panting out loud with each breath.

He loved doing this to her, loved getting her all soaked and hot.

"Honey... so good..."

"Mmm," he responded, sucking gently on her nub while lightly pinching her nipples.

Jade's legs started to tremble. Then with a loud cry, her whole body convulsed.

Argh, that was so hot. He needed her now. He got up and looked for his wallet to get a condom. Then realisation hit.

"Oh, shit."

"What's wrong?" Jade asked, looking flushed and beautiful against the window, blue skies and the city skyline behind her.

"I don't have a condom on me."

Jade giggled. "But you've always been prepared."

"I haven't had a need for it since we broke up," he said with a frown.

Jade could make him come with her hands and mouth, but he'd been dying to be inside her. Maybe he could withdraw when—

"You have a clean bill of health, right?" Jade asked.

"Of course, baby. I've always been careful."

"I went on the pill when I started seeing you."

He grinned, relief washing over him. "And you're still on it, right?"

"Uh-huh," she said.

"In that case…" He stalked to where she was and positioned himself between her legs.

"I'm glad I don't have to miss out on this," he murmured, running the tip of his erection on her nub.

"I'm glad, too," Jade said breathlessly.

He rained kisses on her face and neck while he continued to rub her clit with his cock, building her next arousal.

It wasn't long before Jade's hips were undulating against him.

He sought her entrance and pushed in.

They moaned together, revelling in the most intimate of connections.

"Jade, you feel incredible, sweetheart," he grunted as he tried to go slow. He wanted to savour this, wanted to prolong the delicious skin-to-skin friction, wanted to drown for as long as he could in her welcoming wetness.

But before long he was driving into her faster, unable to help himself.

"Yes… Lucas… yes," Jade panted, grasping his shoulders and meeting his thrusts.

He lost all control. He clutched her hips and pounded, straining from his efforts.

"Lucas!" Jade called out, her body clenching tightly around his cock.

With that he erupted inside her, his eyesight dimming from the force of his release.

CHAPTER TWENTY-ONE

Ten months later…

"Yay!" Jade said to Lexie, clapping, as her friend sat back down on her chair.

"I can't believe I won it," Lexie said with a laugh. "I was sure Rick had it in the bag."

"Wanna swap?" Rick teased. "My expensive bottle of Carmichael Cabernet Sauvignon for your gift certificate."

"I'm surprised you want to part with that," Lexie said. "Isn't it special, with only a small number of bottles produced every few years or so?"

"Yes, it's special. But I'm hoping to score one from my cousins."

"Oh, of course," Lexie said, blushing. "I guess when it's your cousins' own wine label, you can always get one."

"Not always," Rick said. "Sometimes they're so limited that they can't just give them away to anyone who asks."

"I'd say you're lucky you won it, Rick," Lucas said. "When I asked the brothers if I could buy one as a runner-up prize for our Halloween dinner pantomime, they happily donated that bottle. But I couldn't get another one even if I wanted to pay for it. They were all gone."

"Oh. I better keep this then," Rick said. "Sorry, Lexie. In a few years, this wine could be worth more than the amount of your gift certificate."

"Aw, you're not gonna swap with me? I was going to," Lexie said with a cute pout.

Jade glanced at Lucas, giving him a meaningful look. Lexie had been flirting with Rick more and more. But unfortunately, Rick was so used to getting that kind of attention from women that he simply hadn't noticed how Lexie had become more overt.

"Everyone." Thomas Bilton's voice boomed through the speakers. "Before we get our wonderful DJ to start playing the dance music, my son, Lucas, wants to say a few words."

Jade raised her eyebrows. Lucas hadn't told her anything about speaking in front of everybody today.

She smiled as Bilton Machineries employees and business partners gave Lucas a thunderous applause as he made his way to the stage.

It had astounded everyone when Thomas announced his true relationship with Lucas at last year's staff Christmas party. The moment was touching and poignant, with father and son standing side by side on the stage, both vowing to continue the company culture that had fostered productivity and creativity.

In a moving moment that had brought copious tears to Jade's eyes, Lucas had paid tribute not only to Thomas, but also to Diana, his stepmother. He'd said that without Diana's contributions, Bilton Machineries couldn't be the success that it was now. It was a humble, heart-rending speech that had every person up on their feet and dabbing the corners of their eyes.

And here was Lucas again, up on the same stage. Jade wondered what her boyfriend was about to say.

"Hello, everybody," he started. "I promise not to make you cry tonight."

Someone cheered and the audience laughed.

"Just over twelve months ago, my life changed. Most of you here already know the story, but what I haven't shared yet was how it all started."

Silence cloaked the room, the air filling with anticipation.

"Until that point in time, I wasn't prepared to listen to a single word Thomas Bilton had to say. I avoided him at all costs. I detested him." Lucas said.

Jade's eyes filled. She knew what he was talking about.

"If it weren't for one particular moment, things would have been very different," Lucas continued. "I wouldn't have known the love of my father and the support of my new family. My mother would still be looking over her shoulder, her heart holding on to some misplaced anger. And I would have been just plodding along in life—missing out on the greatest, sweetest love I've ever known."

Tears flowed down Jade's cheeks. Damn him. Why didn't he warn her about this speech so she could have prepared herself?

"That moment was when this beautiful, blushing woman asked me to read Thomas Bilton's letter. 'Please, just read it', she said, because her boss expected her to come back with my answer. I was mad at her then. I

225

thought I'd been manipulated. But I did read the letter for no reason other than... well... I couldn't say no to her. Just couldn't say no. So ladies and gentlemen, please raise your glasses to the irresistible Jade Tully."

"To the irresistible Jade Tully," everyone said, holding their wine glasses up.

Jade flushed furiously, smiling through her tears. How embarrassing!

"Aw, honey," Lucas said, looking at her. "I made you cry."

"You said you weren't going to make anyone cry tonight," she called out.

"Come up here," Lucas said.

What?

"Go, Jade!" Rick cheered, clapping. Then everyone else was clapping with Rick, encouraging her to join Lucas.

With a sigh, she got up.

"Here, take these," Lexie said, handing her some tissues.

"Thanks," she said, then made her way to her boyfriend. Sure, this was sweet and all, but he'd still have to pay for this later.

When she reached him, Lucas put an arm around her and kissed her temple. A chorus of 'aww' and 'how sweet' filled the room.

Lucas went back to the microphone. "Last year, I won a prize for being runner-up in the pantomime contest. Jade chose the item herself, and I know it means a lot to her. Dad said back then that it was something to give to the woman of my dreams. Well, here she is, and I've been waiting for the perfect moment to present it to her."

Lucas took a box from his pocket.

"You said you gave it to your mum," she whispered.

"I only said that so you wouldn't keep asking about it," he said.

She smiled, thrilled to be getting *her* necklace back. It was even more special that Lucas was giving it to her.

"Thank you," she said as she took the box from him.

"Open it," he encouraged.

She untied the bow wrapped around the box and lifted the lid. More tears rushed to her eyes and she pressed her hands to her lips to stop herself from sobbing.

The necklace lay in the velvet box. But in the middle, where the heart-shaped hole was, sat a large and very beautiful diamond ring.

Lucas knelt down on one knee. "I love you so much, Jade. You've captured my heart from the very first moment we met. I can't imagine living the rest of my life without you. Will you marry me, please?"

She tried to control her silent sobbing. "Yes," she managed to croak out.

The room erupted in rapturous applause. With cheers and whistles from the audience, Lucas put the ring on her finger, then he stood up and clasped the necklace around her neck.

With heart bursting, she kissed him, not caring that everyone was watching.

*

227

"Hey, are you two forgetting you're at a company party?"

Jade stopped kissing Lucas and smiled at Lexie. "No. We just thought that since we just got engaged, no one would mind if we kissed while everyone else danced."

"Be honest, babe," Lucas drawled. "You really just wanted a good snog right now."

She rolled her eyes. Yes, it was true. She didn't want to wait until they got home to get a proper, long kiss from her new fiancé.

Lexie chuckled. "Oh, Jade, how you've changed from being flustered around Lucas to not having a care in the world if you get caught making out with him in public."

"Hey, we weren't making out," she said with a laugh. "And this isn't exactly public. This is a private party."

Lexie shook her head good-naturedly.

"Drinks!" Rick said, approaching them with his limited edition Carmichael wine.

"You opened the bottle?" Lucas asked.

"Of course. When else would you consume a wine like this but on special occasions? We just need to be quiet so others won't notice. There's not enough for everyone. Ah, here are the glasses."

A waiter placed a tray of crystal wine glasses on their table.

"You know," Jade said as Rick poured. "No one won the bet on who was going to be captured by love first among you bachelors."

"I know," Rick said. "Who'd think that Lucas would be the next guy to come off the market?"

"That sounded like an interesting bet," Lexie piped in.

"Yeah," Jade said. "No one bet on Lucas because they all thought he'd be last."

"Well, they were all wrong, weren't they?" Lucas murmured, pulling Jade to him and kissing her hair. "I heard, though, that they're starting a new round."

"Really?" Jade asked. "Who's got the shortest odds?"

"Simon, I think," Lucas said. "And yet again, no one bet for Rick."

Rick laughed. "Smart women."

"Can anyone join?" Lexie asked, grinning. "I bet you'll be next, Rick."

"What makes you think that?" Rick asked with an incredulous laugh.

"Because sometimes the most unexpected answer is the most obvious," Lexie said.

"I've never heard of that line before," Rick said. "But I'm sure I couldn't be next, because the unexpected just doesn't occur regularly enough."

Lexie paused to consider Rick's words. "I'd still bet on you."

Rick smirked. "It's your money, Lexie. I warned you."

Jade snuggled closer to Lucas. "I think Lexie will win this bet," she whispered in his ear.

Lucas chuckled. "Really, sweetheart? You don't know Rick as well as I do. There's a good reason why he wants to stay single. Lexie's chances are super slim."

"What's the reason?"

Lucas shook his head. "I love you and I trust you. But I'm afraid I'm not at liberty to say," he said in a serious tone.

"Really? Hmm. Intriguing. But I have a good feeling about Lexie's prospects of winning." She might be biased, but she knew that once Lexie had made up her mind about a guy, he had little hope of resisting.

"No. Rick won't be the next to fall," Lucas said, sounding certain.

"You want to put your money where your mouth is?"

"Sure, babe," Lucas said with a grin. Then he leaned in to whisper. "But I bet we both know where I want to put my mouth right now."

Jade blushed. Ah, she couldn't wait to be alone with him.

Thank you for reading!

Rick and Lexie's love story is next. *The Unyielding Bachelor (Captured by Love, Book 2)* is released in May 2015.

*

Lucas first appeared in the book *Again*, Book 3 of the *Time for Love* series, which features the love story of Connor and Amanda. The *Time for Love* series started with one of the Carmichael brothers' romance. Enjoy the first chapter of *Forever (Time for Love, Book 1)* in the next pages.

Forever (Time for Love Book 1) Extract

Rebecca Andrews and Zach Carmichael

CHAPTER ONE

Extremely lucky. How else could Rebecca Andrews describe what she should be feeling for the new work offer she'd recently received? But somehow, she couldn't muster the same excitement that radiated from her friend and colleague Sarah Daley.

"I understand why you're not ecstatic about this, Bec, but I still think you should grab it with both hands," Sarah said, her wide eyes magnifying the intensity of her belief.

Rebecca thanked the server, who placed two mango smoothies on their table, before responding to Sarah. "I know. But the client is *Magda Carmichael*."

"Yes. I know that's a big deal for you. But you love Magda, don't you? She's asked for us. She doesn't want anyone else to go with her."

Sarah, one of Rebecca's four best friends whom she'd known since primary school, had been ready to pack her bags from the moment they got the call from their nursing agency. They had both been personally selected by Magda Carmichael—a very wealthy and absolutely sweet lady—to be her private nurses during her month-long holiday aboard one of the most luxurious cruise ships in the world.

"You have to go with me, Bec," Sarah pleaded. "We've both never been on a cruise before, and we'll get to visit some exotic Asian cities. It'll be fun!"

"Fun?" Rebecca said with a laugh. "We're not being hired to have fun. We're being hired to work, remember?"

"I know. But we won't be working twenty-four/seven. That's why they want the two of us there, so we could work on shifts looking after Magda. We'll still have some private time to enjoy what promises to be an incredible trip."

"I do wonder why she needs two nurses with her?" Rebecca mused. "She'd fully recovered from her hip replacement surgery, and according to the agency, she's not currently suffering from any illness or injury."

"She's almost eighty, Bec. Magda and her family probably prefer to have two professionals with her on the cruise in case something happens. Besides, she could very well afford to pay for our salary *and* our trip."

Yes, the Carmichaels could certainly afford those and much more. Magda Carmichael's late husband was a self-made multi-millionaire who'd founded The Carmichael Corporation, one of the biggest property development companies in Australia. Now Magda's three grandsons looked after the various interests of the company, which extended to wineries and eco-tourism.

"I wonder who else would be accompanying her apart from nursing staff?" Rebecca asked. "I'm sure she wouldn't be going on a holiday like that by herself."

"You mean you want to know if Zach will be going," Sarah said softly. "You said you're over him."

"I am. But that doesn't mean I want to bump into him again," she responded, ignoring the pinching in her chest that still happened every time she thought of Zachary Carmichael, Magda's oldest grandson.

"It's none of our business and it would be rude to ask. Besides, I can't imagine Zach accompanying his grandmother on a cruise for a month even if he's very fond of her." Sarah leaned across the table with a serious look. "Bec, you know it's time you let go of whatever feelings you still feel for Zach—even the bitterness and regret. And do you really want to say no to Magda?"

Rebecca sighed. Magda Carmichael was the nicest, kindest, most generous client she'd ever worked with. When she and Sarah were hired as Magda's physical rehabilitation nurses while Magda recovered from her hip replacement surgery after an accidental slip in her bathroom, Magda had treated them like family, not paid personnel. She'd often wondered if the fact that Magda didn't have granddaughters was the reason she'd grown attached to her and Sarah. At twenty-eight, both she and Sarah were close to the ages of Magda's three grandsons. Zach was the oldest at thirty-two. His younger brothers Jeffrey and Gregory were thirty and twenty-nine.

"You know I can't say no to Magda," she admitted.

"Yay! You have to tell the agency you're accepting the job, then you have to advise Magda's personal assistant that you're going so she can arrange your travel documents," Sarah said excitedly. "I've already emailed her my details that she's asked for."

"Okay. I'll email her when I get home."

"Make sure you do it as soon as you walk through your door. The ship leaves in ten days. I'm sure she'd need time to organise everything."

"Don't worry, I will," she said with a laugh.

"Hey, girls!"

Rebecca and Sarah greeted their three other best friends Brenna Ward, Amanda Payne and Gemma Aldwin with a kiss on their cheeks.

"You look super excited, Sarah. What's up?" Brenna asked.

Sarah gleefully told the newcomers their news.

"Oh my God!" Gemma exclaimed. "I really, really should go back into private nursing. What the hell was I thinking giving it up?"

"You know teaching piano is your main love," Rebecca quipped. "Anyway, if I change my mind about taking it on, you're welcome to take my place."

"Why would you change your mind?" Amanda asked.

"Did I tell you the client is Magda Carmichael?" Sarah interjected.

"Ohh," the other ladies said in unison, their mouths forming a perfect 'O'.

"I see why you're not that keen on this, Bec," Gemma said softly.

Rebecca put on a nonchalant expression. "Well, I very much doubt Zach will be on the cruise. But even if I see him again, so what? It's been seven months since we broke up. Besides, it didn't take him long to replace me with Miss Universe-Australia."

Her eyes stung. Damn it. She should be over the whole thing by now. Why was she so slow in moving on?

"Hey," Brenna said softly, running a comforting hand on her arm. "He's not worth one salty tear, remember?"

She nodded, trying to regain composure. It was hard to stay unaffected when talking about Zach—the only man she'd ever loved. They'd had an incredible four-month relationship that had started not long after she and Sarah were hired to help Magda recover from her surgery.

It was a passionate affair that they'd kept under wraps. The Carmichaels were a favourite subject for gossip magazines and paparazzi, and privacy had become something the family guarded with jealousy. Plus, while there were no written rules about dating relatives of clients, Rebecca's nursing agency would have frowned if they found out she was dating a Carmichael. She loved her job and didn't want to jeopardise it.

Unwanted memories of the moment when she'd told Zach she loved him filled her mind. Yes, it was more than silly of her to expect an 'I love you' back from him, but when he hadn't said it, she'd been so shattered.

She did try to contain her disappointment from his lack of response, understanding that saying 'I love you' wasn't something someone like Zach would say willy-nilly. But she'd gotten scared. According to some of the articles about him, he had a habit of changing girlfriends every six months or so. Somehow, she'd managed to convince herself that Zach was preparing to dump her.

Her friends had suggested that she had a fear of abandonment that stemmed from her childhood experiences with her parents. That was probably true. But knowing that didn't stop her from acting out of fear. She'd decided to break up with Zach before he could do it to her.

Zach had tried to make her change her mind and had said he just needed more time to figure out his feelings. But all his words had done was prove to her that Zach had only enjoyed her as a sexual partner. He didn't *love* her, and it was simply too painful and scary for her to stay with him with that belief.

She frowned at the pain emanating from her chest. Crazy how she still hurt after all the time that had passed. But lingering regret about her actions kept her tethered to thoughts of what might have been.

"Are you okay, Bec?" Sarah asked worriedly.

"Yeah," she lied.

Brenna shook her head. "We know that look on your face. It's called remorse. How many times do we have to tell you that you did the right thing?"

"Breaking up with the man I was dating because he wasn't ready to say 'I love you' back to me?" Rebecca said wryly. "Yeah, great move. I should have been more patient."

"But what you did was totally understandable."

"What if all I had to do was wait a little bit longer? He wouldn't have asked me to go on a business trip with him if he hadn't cared about me, would he?"

"Haven't we had this conversation many times before?" Sarah asked with an eye roll. "Have you forgotten that just one week after you've told him it was over, he'd started dating Miss Universe-Australia?"

Rebecca sniffed as she recalled the magazine article that claimed Miss Universe-Australia was dating one of Sydney's most eligible bachelors—Zachary Carmichael. There were even photos of them in a restaurant, and another while they were coming out of a theatre, with the woman's hand tightly holding on to Zach's arm.

No, it hadn't taken him long to replace her.

"You girls are right. I should stop beating myself up for what I did. For all I know, it saved me from a worse heartbreak that would be harder to recover from."

Thank God that apart from her best friends, no one else knew about her past relationship with Zach. She doubted Zach would have told anyone. She was just a fun diversion to him—as his actions had proven.

She was especially grateful that Magda had no idea about it. She was sure Magda wouldn't have asked for her services if she'd found out.

"Zach's moved on, Bec. Seriously, it's time you did too," Brenna said gently.

"Yes," she said with conviction. To show her friends she meant it, she picked up her phone and called the nursing agency to let them know she was available to work for Magda Carmichael.

*

"You girls have to pack some cocktail dresses," Gemma said. "Let's go shopping tomorrow. At least the three of us who'd be left here on land can share some of the excitement with you before we wallow in jealousy."

"Great idea," Sarah said.

"You'll want new swimsuits as well," Amanda said. "Get a couple of really sexy ones. You never know who you might meet in those places."

"Hey, we're there to work!" Rebecca exclaimed with a laugh.

"Doesn't hurt to be prepared. You'll kick yourself if you bump into a hunk there and you don't have anything sexy with you. And remember our group New Year's resolution?"

"Yes," Rebecca answered with an eye roll.

"Say it," Gemma said.

Rebecca sighed theatrically. "This year, all five of us will make time for love. We won't let our busy schedules or other lame excuses get in the way of making the first move on hot, decent men who aren't afraid of long-term commitment. I still don't know where we'll find them, though," she added sceptically.

"Remind me again why we made that stupid resolution?" Brenna asked.

"First, because we were crazy-drunk," Gemma said with a laugh. "And second, because it's been five New Year's Eves in a row that all five of us didn't have anyone to kiss at the stroke of midnight. And don't forget we've pinky-promised on this."

"Anyone already on your radar, girls?" Rebecca asked curiously.

Her friends shook their heads.

"We still have eleven months to go before the next New Year's Eve," Amanda said.

"And remember, the whole point is for us to *make an effort* instead of sitting on our butts waiting for them to fall on our laps," Sarah said.

"And not letting our exes or painful pasts get in the way," Gemma said, looking pointedly at Rebecca. "It's all about moving forward to find our happily ever after."

They all nodded in agreement.

Rebecca was actually glad of this pact she'd made with her four best friends. It was giving her the much-needed push and motivation to move on from Zach. She loathed to admit it, even to herself, but a big part of her still pined for him constantly.

Well, no use crying over something she couldn't undo. She'd try to give herself—and love—another chance. She'd start dating again and finally push Zach away from her heart and mind. It was about time she did.

*****

"Hi Granny."

"Zach! I'm so glad you could join me for dinner tonight, dear." Magda put down her cup of tea and motioned for Zach to bend down to her.

Zach kissed Magda and sat beside her. "Unfortunately I have things to finish off tonight so I'm just here to say hello. Are you looking forward to the start of your month-long eightieth birthday celebration tomorrow?"

"Of course. I'm so excited I probably won't be able to sleep tonight. And I'm glad you're going with me, Zach. You've been working far too hard lately. You deserve a break."

Zach laughed. "I'm young and energetic, Gran. You don't need to worry about me. But I want to let you know I can't stay for the whole month. I'll be disembarking in Hong Kong in two weeks."

"What? Why can't you stay for the whole month? I thought you would."

"I have work to do and important meetings to attend, Gran," he said in a contrite voice.

"Why can't you do your work from the ship? I was assured electronic communication from there would be reliable wherever in the world we are."

"The coverage might be patchy if we're at sea," he reasoned. "Besides, Jeff and Greg will join us from the Philippines so there's a few days when we're all together before I leave. You know it's not a good idea for the three of us to be absent from the company at the same time for long periods."

"Zachary, just because you're the CEO of our company, and Jeff is the CFO and Greg the COO, those titles shouldn't stop you boys from being my grandsons. I'm already disappointed that your brothers won't be joining me for the whole duration of this trip, but I thought *you* were. You haven't had a single day's break for months! This is the first time I've seen you in weeks and I was hoping the cruise was my opportunity to spend some time with you," Magda said a little tremulously.

Zach pressed his lips, guilt eating at him. Spending time with her grandsons brought Magda the joy and comfort their family's wealth couldn't give. He knew that for all of his grandmother's exuberance and resilience of spirit, she still acutely mourned the loss of her husband, her only son, and her daughter-in-law. Heck, even he still missed his grandfather and his parents terribly. That horrific light plane accident two years ago that had cruelly robbed them of three people they loved dearly was not something any of them would ever forget. And special occasions like Magda's eightieth birthday always brought back the best and worst of the memories.

He rubbed his chin, wavering in his decision to make the trip short. The weekly phone calls, he knew, didn't make up for his recent physical absence.

"Okay, Gran," he said, grasping Magda's hand. "I'll make arrangements so I can do my work on board the ship and stay with you for the whole month."

"Oh, thank you, Zach. I do miss you, you know," Magda said delightedly.

"I know," he responded as he got up. "I have to go and tidy up a few things before we leave tomorrow."

"Okay. Make sure you're free to join us for dinner tomorrow night—our first night on the ship."

"Who's 'us', by the way?"

"Well, there's your Grand-Auntie Miriam," Magda responded.

Zach nodded, not minding the thought of spending time with Magda's younger sister.

"And I've invited Phillip Lee."

Zach hid his grimace, not looking forward to socialising with the man. Phillip had been the bearer of hurtful news that Zach would rather forget, and lately, he'd been noticing repressed antagonism from Phillip directed toward him.

But Phillip's late mother was Magda's best friend, and Phillip was someone that Magda considered a nephew even though he wasn't blood related.

"That's very surprising that you've asked him to come," he commented casually.

"I felt sorry for him," Magda said with a sigh. "Did you know that the company he worked for went bankrupt a month ago?"

241

"Yes, I've heard about that," Zach said. Phillip had been hounding him and his brothers for a job at The Carmichael Corporation.

"Well, he was telling me the other day how lost and lonely he felt. So I asked him to join us. I'm paying for his expenses."

Zach simply nodded. His grandmother had a heart of gold.

"I've also invited my friends Olga and Debra to join us on this trip," Magda continued. "Their granddaughters are accompanying them."

This time, Zach couldn't help groaning out loud. He'd bet the granddaughter Debra was bringing with her was Vicky—a woman he'd had sex with four times in the last couple of months.

It was Vicky who'd offered a casual liaison agreement with him, since neither of them was interested in a committed relationship. But lately, she'd started to ask him out to dinners and events. He'd been quick to decline, reminding her of how it was between them. He wasn't interested in anything long-term with Vicky and didn't want her to have misconceptions.

At least Vicky was being as tight-lipped as he was about their arrangement. He could just imagine how their grandmothers would enthusiastically embrace the possibility of their grandkids married off to each other if they knew. He shuddered at the thought.

"Don't even think about pairing me off with anyone while on this trip, Grandmother," he warned.

Magda laughed at his tone. "If you insist."

"Oh, I insist, Gran."

"Fine, I won't," Magda said readily.

"Good. I'll see you tomorrow."

"Okay, Zach. By the way, my nurses will also be joining us for the trip."

"Your nurses?" Zach asked in surprise.

"Yes. Even though I'm fit and well, you never know what might happen while we're at sea. Better that they're on hand."

His heart hammered in his chest. "Who... uh... have I met these nurses before?"

"Yes. Rebecca and Sarah. They're those lovely girls who helped me recover from my hip replacement. You remember them, don't you?"

He paled.

Rebecca. She was going to be there. On the ship. With him. For a month.

"Don't tell me you can't remember them, Zach. They looked after me for six months."

He roused himself from his shock. "Sure, I remember them. I'll... uh... see you tomorrow."

Forever (Time for Love Book 1) now available.

BOOK LINKS AND OTHERS

Be the first to know about my new releases and updates:
Subscribe to my newsletter:
http://mirandapcharles.com/subscribe/

Review Request:
I hope you enjoyed this book. Please consider leaving a review, short or long, on the site from which you got your copy. Reviews from readers help books get discovered by others :).
Thank you,
Miranda xxx

Connect with me (I would really love to hear from you):
Like and message me from my Facebook page:
facebook.com/MirandaPCharles
Or follow and send me a tweet on Twitter:
twitter.com/MirandaPCharles
You can also email me at mirandapcharles@gmail.com.

My Other Books:

Lifestyle by Design Series
Book 1: **Will To Love**
Clarise Carson and Will Matthews
Book 2: **Heart Robber**
Jessa Allen and Rob Granger
Book 3: **Ray of Love**
Faye Summers and Ray Thackery

Secret Dreams Series
Book 1: **Secret Words**
Jasmine Allen and Kane Summers
Book 2: **Secret Designs**
Ari Mitchell and Dylan Summers
Book 3: **Secret Moves**
Kris McCann and Trey Andrews
Book 4: **Secret Tastes**
Samantha Lane and Adam Craig

Time for Love Series
Book 1: **Forever**
Rebecca Andrews and Zach Carmichael
Book 2: **Finally**
Sarah Daley and Jeff Carmichael
Book 3: **Again**
Amanda Payne and Connor Reid
Book 4: **Always**
Brenna Ward and Ash Payne
Book 5: **At Last**
Gemma Aldwyn and Greg Carmichael

Captured by Love Series
Book 1: The Unwilling Executive
Lucas Renner and Jade Tully
Book 2: The Unyielding Bachelor - available May 2015
Rick Donnelly and Lexie Mead

Again, thank you, thank you, thank you.
Miranda P. Charles

9 781508 684664